READY FOR TROUBLE

When Clay Overman is shot at he suspects the worst; he has no idea who wants him dead. Then the stream, supplying water for the Bar O ranch, runs dry. Scheming men are intent on robbing him and his father of their ranch and their lives. In this lawless world everyone must fight to retain their possessions and Clay is ready for trouble. But when the shooting begins his life will be on the line until the last shot . . .

Books by Corba Sunman
in the Linford Western Library:

RANGE WOLVES
LONE HAND
GUN TALK
TRIGGER LAW
GUNSMOKE JUSTICE
BIG TROUBLE
GUN PERIL
SHOWDOWN AT SINGING SPRINGS
TWISTED TRAIL
RAVEN'S FEUD
FACES IN THE DUST
MARSHAL LAW
ARIZONA SHOWDOWN
THE LONG TRAIL
SHOOT-OUT AT OWL CREEK
RUNNING CROOKED
HELL'S COURTYARD
KILL OR BE KILLED

CORBA SUNMAN

READY FOR TROUBLE

Complete and Unabridged

LINFORD
Leicester

First published in Great Britain in 2009 by
Robert Hale Limited
London

First Linford Edition
published 2010
by arrangement with
Robert Hale Limited
London

British Library CIP Data

Sunman, Corba.
 Ready for trouble. - -
 (Linford western library)
 1. Western stories.
 2. Large type books.
 I. Title II. Series
 823.9'2–dc22

 ISBN 978–1–44480–361–7

Published by
F. A. Thorpe (Publishing)
Anstey, Leicestershire
Set by Words & Graphics Ltd.
Anstey, Leicestershire
Printed and bound in Great Britain by
T. J. International Ltd., Padstow, Cornwall

This book is printed on acid-free paper

1

As he followed the dried-up stream that was supposed to water the Bar O ranch in Morgan County, Arizona, Clay Overman was keenly aware that trouble was looming. His blue eyes narrowed as he let his thoughts and suspicions have full rein. Although he could not put his finger on the source of his concern, he knew his assumption was correct. Too many incidents had occurred in the past two weeks — minor problems that did not amount to much individually, but, when viewed together, added up to an ominous score, and he was worried because his father, Pete Overman, refused to heed the signs that trouble was moving in on them.

Tall in the saddle, broad-shouldered and powerfully built, Clay's eyes were pale blue, his long hair almost yellow. There were slight hollows in his cheeks and not an ounce of spare flesh anywhere on his big frame. He was wearing range clothes — a red shirt under a leather vest, faded Levi's and batwing chaps, light-brown riding boots adorned with plain spurs, and a weathered grey Stetson with a turned-down brim. He carried a Winchester .44–40 in a saddle boot and wore a .45 Colt six-gun in a holster snug against his right hip.

His keen gaze flickered to cover his surroundings as he rode towards Water Canyon. In the previous week he had been shot at from cover, and although he had found a stranger's tracks on Bar O grass he had been unable to discover the identity of his assailant. Now he rode with his hand close to the butt of his pistol and a deadly alertness rampant in his mind. Someone was trying to scare him off the range, if not kill him, but the culprit would have to come out into the open before long and then there could be an accounting.

He twisted in his saddle to view his

back trail. The sun was almost overhead, burning with the ferocity of high summer, and he cuffed back his Stetson and wiped sweat from his forehead. The undulating range stretched away to mountains in the west which were purpled by distance. When he discovered no movement anywhere he returned his attention to the dried-up stream, which had been running with water the day before. His expression was laced with anger as he considered that someone or something must have blocked the water course during the night, and it looked as if he would have to ride all the way into Water Canyon to locate the source of the problem.

He rode on, heading north, and his thoughts switched to more personal matters. His teeth clicked together when he thought of Sue Truscott, the only daughter of Big Frank Truscott, who ran more than a thousand head of steers on the sprawling FT ranch. Sue had been sweet on Clay ever since they were at school together, and over the years he had fought off all opposition to their relationship, until he had got to an age when he realized that he had nothing to offer a girl like Sue except a life of hard work and near-poverty.

Sue had always been full of big ideas for their future. She stood to inherit FT when Big Frank cashed his chips, but Clay had his own dreams, which did not include taking on another man's estate and living on a product which was not of his own making. He wanted to establish his own holdings, as Big Frank had done in his time, and he had slowly frozen Sue out until she turned away from him, patently hurt by his changing attitude. They were civil enough whenever they met, but he was keenly aware of the chasm he had wrought between them, and Sue's eyes were never without a glint of bewilderment these days.

Clay thrust out his jaw as he looked ahead. He was ready for trouble, but so far there was nothing but a dark shadow hanging over him, and the tension was beginning to get to him. He touched spurs to his sorrel and sent the animal on at a faster pace, wishing he could be in two places at once because he was afraid that something bad might happen to his father while they were apart, for the older man refused to believe trouble was stalking them.

A further three hours of riding through rising, broken ground took Clay into wild country, and he loosened his pistol in its holster as he continued. He had hunted through this area many times; knew it intimately, and was making for high ground which would give him a glimpse far ahead of the meandering water course he was following. At length he left the sorrel, took a pair of field-glasses from his saddle-bag, drew his Winchester from its boot, and ascended copper-coloured rocks.

It took him an hour to reach the summit of the bluff, and he lay for some minutes, breathing heavily; sweating profusely, until his tortured body regained its composure. Impatience dragged him up and he went forward to peer down the reverse slope in the direction of Water Canyon. Now the winding water course lay exposed to his keen gaze and he cuffed sweat from his forehead and eyes and adjusted his field-glasses to study the stream.

He saw immediately why the water had stopped flowing on to Bar O range. It had been blocked at a narrow point and diverted into a shallow gully off to the east. He gazed at the dam while considering the situation. Cottonwoods had been felled in a nearby copse, cut into logs and piled across the flow of the water, and stakes had been hammered into position to hold them in place. Earth had been thrown against the logs on the downstream side to effectively block the natural water course.

Using his glasses, he studied the whole area, looking for movement but seeing nothing untoward, and when his shock had receded he sighed and made the laborious descent to his sorrel, his thoughts sombre as he wondered what was going on.

His keen gaze was intent on the ground as he approached the dam and his eyes narrowed when he saw a profusion of tracks around the area. He reined in and again subjected the terrain to a meticulous search. He saw where tracks led into and out of a nearby copse and kept his right hand close to the butt of his holstered pistol as he read the signs. At least three riders had been present when the dam was built.

He dismounted, trailed his reins, and stood looking at the dam. Someone had gone to a lot of trouble to deny Bar O its water supply. He studied the build-up of water behind the dam and noted where it had been diverted into a gully to follow the lie of the land to the east. In his mind he could see the range stretching in that direction and compressed his lips when he thought of the nesters who had moved into that part of the range over the past months.

Clay knew it was against the law to divert any stream from its natural course. But the law was weak in Morgan County. Sheriff Bill Cooper operated out of Sunset Ridge, the county seat to the west of Pine Flats, where a deputy sheriff, Snape Ritter, controlled the law in the little cow town. Cooper was a serious type who always went through the motions of law dealing but with little success, while Ritter seemed to have his own interests in mind whenever he handled law business.

Clay turned his attention to the dam. He grasped the top log, lifted one end clear of the retaining stakes, and threw it aside. A trickle of water seeped into the piled earth in front of the obstruction as he took hold of a second log. He had to exert his strength to lift it out of position, and was breathing hard when it was clear of the stream. Water began pouring through the piled earth, beating it down to resume its original course.

There were a dozen logs in the dam, and Clay stood thigh deep in water by the time he had removed the last of them. The thrust of the pent-up water being released almost knocked him off balance. He waded to the bank, climbed clear of the current, and sat down to take off his boots and empty them of water. He was pulling them on again when he heard the click of a steel-shod hoof against a stone, and whirled to face the sound, his right hand dropping to the butt of his pistol.

A rider was sitting on a brown horse only yards away, having emerged from the nearby copse — a hard-faced young man wearing travel-stained range clothes that had seen better days. His brown eyes were screwed up against the glare of the sun and the big pistol in his right hand was steady, its black muzzle pointed at Clay's chest.

'It took us hours to build that dam last night,' the man said harshly. 'What for did you take it apart?'

'Why did you build it?' Clay countered.

'Ain't that plain? Me and my pards were paid to set the stream flowing in another direction. Someone figured it would be better running east than south.'

'Not for me. My pa and me ranch south of here and rely on this water for our stock. Don't you know it's against the law to block or divert a stream?'

'There is only one law here and this is it.' The man waggled his gun. 'Put your hands up. Give me trouble and you're dead, mister.'

Clay considered his chances before lifting his hands shoulder high, aware that he could not resist a levelled gun. The stranger dismounted and came forward, his gun hand jammed against his right hip, the muzzle gaping steadily at Clay.

'Turn around,' he rasped, 'and keep your hands high.'

Clay obeyed and felt his pistol being removed from his holster.

'Who paid you to build the dam?' Clay asked. 'Who are you working for?'

'Not the sodbusters. They ain't got a red cent between them.' The man laughed. 'Don't fret about who my boss is. I'll take you to him and he'll decide what's to be done with you. I've been told to watch out for a guy named Clay Overman, and I'm guessing that's who you are. I heard you're hell on wheels at the drop of a hat, so don't give me trouble. I'll shoot you dead soon as blink if you try anything.'

'I'm Clay Overman of the Big O ten miles south of here.' Clay dropped his hands and turned to face his captor. 'So what happens now?'

'You'll rebuild the dam while I sit and watch you.' The man's lips stretched into a grin. 'I don't envy you the chore. It near broke my back last night, but we had to cut down the trees before we could start so you're a step ahead of us. Now get to it. I want that water blocked off again, and don't try any tricks unless you wanta finish up on

11

your face with the dam sitting on your back.'

Clay stifled a sigh as he began to drag the logs back into the stream. He found it hard work, but with the pistol covering his every movement there was nothing he could do except obey the gunman's harsh instructions. When he paused after an hour's work to protest that he needed tools in order to continue, the man whistled shrilly and waved an arm in the direction of the copse. Clay stared in surprise when a wagon pulled by two horses rolled into view from the trees and came towards the dam.

Two men were on the driving seat of the vehicle; their saddle horses tied behind. Both were grinning as they halted by the stream, and one rummaged in the back of the wagon before tossing out a long-handled sodbuster and a sledge-hammer. They were hard-faced men and looked as if they were living rough on the range.

'He works real good, Shorty,' one of

them observed. 'Keep him at it. I don't feel like rebuilding that dam. What for did he pull it down?'

'Said he didn't like the direction the water was flowing in when we changed its course.' Shorty grinned and waggled his pistol at Clay. 'Get on with it. Sim, it is your turn to cook grub and make coffee, and after we've eaten you two can head on back to the shack. I'm gonna be here a long time yet, by the look of it.'

Clay picked up the hammer and drove some of the stakes into the bed of the stream to hold the logs in place. He was ready to resist should the opportunity arise, but the man with the gun was taking no chances and did not relax his vigilance. An hour passed and the aroma of cooking food assailed his nostrils to make him aware of hunger, but the trio ate the food and drank the coffee without offering him any.

The two men with the wagon departed soon after finishing their meal and headed west. Clay stiffened himself for action as he continued rebuilding the dam. Shorty sat on a knoll close by the stream, his pistol covering Clay, but the heat of the sun, combined with the meal he had eaten, seemed to take the edge off his alertness and Clay noted the muzzle of the pistol beginning to droop. He took a tighter grip on the long handle of the sodbuster and eased furtively towards his captor while digging dirt and tossing it in front of the logs.

'OK, that should do it,' Shorty declared at length, and Clay looked up to see the man pushing himself to his feet, his gun hand dropping to his side as he moved.

Clay reacted swiftly. He swung the sodbuster and lunged forward, aiming the shining blade of the tool at Shorty's gun hand. A metallic clang sounded as the blade smacked against the pistol. Shorty uttered a yell, dropped the weapon and clutched at his hand. Clay swung the sodbuster again, this time connecting with Shorty's head, and the man slumped forward into the water building up behind the dam. Clay dropped the tool, leaned forward to grab Shorty by the scruff of the neck, and dragged him spluttering out of the stream.

Shorty was helpless on his hands and knees while Clay picked up the pistol that had been dropped. When Shorty recovered his breath he looked up to find himself staring into the muzzle of his own gun, and he shrugged fatalistically in acceptance of the situation.

'You know what you're gonna do right now, don't you?' Clay demanded.

'Take the dam apart!' Shorty surmised.

'Damn right!' Clay nodded. 'And don't take all day about it. When you've done that I'm gonna hustle you into Pine Flats and hand you over to the law.'

'You ain't got no call to do that,' Shorty protested. 'I wasn't gonna shoot you.'

'So tell me about this business and I

just might let you ride out after your pards. What else have you been up to around the county? Was it you shot at me last week? And who paid you to build this dam?'

'I can't rightly tell you.' Shorty shook his head. 'We was paid to do the job and told we'd have to carry the can if anything went wrong. The pay is good so I'll take what's coming to me.'

'If you wanta get out of this jam you're in then you better tell me who paid you to block the stream,' Clay insisted harshly, but Shorty had finished talking.

Clay stood watching intently while Shorty dismantled the dam again. When the water was running clear and free, Clay motioned for Shorty to mount up. They rode out, heading south, following the stream towards Bar O. Shorty rode slightly ahead, his shoulders slumped. Clay maintained silence. His gun was back in its holster and he carried Shorty's pistol in his right hand.

Shadows were closing in by the time they reached the Bar O. Clay sighed with relief when he sighted the ranch buildings. The stream was brimming with water again, and Pete Overman, Clay's father, was standing on the bank of the creek beside the ranch house, watching water cascading in to refill the hollows. Shadows were long on the grass as evening drew on.

Pete was carrying a Winchester in his right hand. He turned to gaze silently at Shorty when he heard the sound of approaching hoofs, and remained silent until Clay had dismounted. Pete Overman was tall and thin, dried out by his years of eking a living out of punching cows in a tough climate. His blue eyes were deep-set under a prominent brow, his face wrinkled; tanned to the colour of old leather. But his shoulders were unbowed as he gazed at Shorty, who, sullen-faced, sat on his horse silently.

'Who is your friend, Clay?' Pete demanded.

'He ain't no friend of mine, Pa,' Clay

replied. 'Last night he built a dam across the stream about a mile this side of Water Canyon.'

Pete listened to Clay's explanation of what had happened at the dam, and the muzzle of his rifle lifted to point at Shorty's chest.

'What for did you do that, mister?' Pete demanded. 'You better have a mighty good reason for blocking my water.'

'He ain't likely to talk, Pa,' Clay said. 'I've questioned him and so far he's kept his lip buttoned. I reckon to take him into Pine Flats and hand him over to the law.'

'Do you reckon Ritter will get anything out of him?' Pete queried. 'You go into the house and get yourself some grub, son, and leave me to talk to this jigger. He ain't leaving my range before he tells me what is going on.'

'Sounds like a good idea.' Clay nodded. 'Get down from that horse, Shorty, and don't make the mistake of trying to get the better of my pa if you wanta see the sun come up in the morning. He can fight his weight in wildcats.'

'Shorty can take care of the horses while I talk to him,' Pete said. 'I need to go into town tomorrow so we can deliver him to the law then, if he's still in one piece.'

Clay stood on the porch for a moment and watched Shorty leading the two horses across the yard to the barn, followed by Pete. He turned to enter the house, but paused when he caught the smell of smoke on the breeze. Alarm was triggered instantly in his mind, for a range fire was the worst of all calamities which could befall a cattle rancher. He turned into the wind and inhaled deeply, then ran along the porch to peer into the distance beyond the house.

Smoke was rising rapidly into the bright sky, an ominous stain that was spreading quickly under the relentless urging of the prevailing wind. Clay gazed transfixed while shock filled him with a cold chill. Then he ran swiftly across the yard, yelling the dread word feared by all ranchers in high summer.

'Fire, Pa!' He yelled. 'There's fire out by Six Acre Bottom.'

Pete turned instantly, his rugged face filling with shock. Clay pushed past his father and snatched the sorrel's reins from Shorty's hands. He swung into his saddle and spurred the horse into action. The horse hit its best pace before reaching the front corner of the house, and Clay gritted his teeth as he rode hell for leather towards the fire, noting that small groups of cattle on the home pasture were already moving uneasily away from the fiery path of the growing conflagration.

Clay became aware that he was riding directly into the centre of the smoke and veered to his left to clear the rapidly advancing line of fire. Smoke was thicker now, choking his lungs with its foul density. He rode clear of it and realized immediately that he was powerless to prevent the spread of the fire. An acre of range was already burning, and the line of the blaze was advancing across the broad sweep of the dry land at an alarming rate.

He reined in clear of the smoke, shaking his head as he judged the direction of the inferno. It looked like the ranch house was doomed, and he spurred the sorrel back towards the ranch yard. If they would save anything from their home then they had to work fast.

Pete was coming towards him, mounted on Shorty's horse, and Clay signalled for his father to turn about and ride clear. The fire was advancing rapidly and it was obvious that they would be unable to salvage anything from the house, and worse, if they did not get out immediately their lives could be forfeit . . .

2

Clay rode in beside his father and they went back to the front of the house. Smoke was blowing ahead of the fire, blotting out the sun and cutting down their vision. Wisps of burning grass were flying through the air. The roof of the house was already smouldering; the tinder-dry woodwork ignited easily and flared. Pete sprang from the horse and started to run into the house. Clay dismounted swiftly and went after his father, grasped his arm and pulled him back.

'Stay out, Pa,' he advised. 'The house will go like a torch when it catches.'

'I've got money and papers in the cache in the big room,' Pete said sharply. 'I can't let them burn.'

'Make it quick then. I'll stay with you.'

They ran into the house and Pete

made straight for the fireplace in the big living room. He pulled a loose flat stone out of the hearth to reveal a cavity, and Clay watched him remove a sheaf of papers. Smoke was already drifting into the house, and Clay could hear the ominous crackle of devouring flames as the roof caught and flared.

'Time to go, Pa,' Clay yelled, and caught Pete's arm as the older man made as if to go through to his bedroom.

Pete shook his head and turned for the front door. They ran out to the porch, and Clay was surprised to see the fire already sweeping through the grass at the side of the house which led down to the creek.

'It's moving faster than a galloping horse,' Pete said angrily, 'and nothing this side of Hell will stop it. Let's get out of here, Clay.'

They ran to their uneasy horses and swung into their saddles.

'Hell, I want to get your mother's

photograph out of the bedroom,' Pete said, reining in. 'It's all I've got left of her, Clay. I've got to fetch it.'

'Sorry, Pa, but you're more important than a photograph.' Clay snatched at his father's reins, spurred his own horse, and led Pete away across the yard. They reined in clear of the conflagration, and Clay, looking back over his shoulder, saw that the roof of the house was now well alight.

'You wouldn't have stood a chance going back in there,' Clay observed. 'Stay clear now, you hear? I'm gonna ride around to where the fire started and see what is going on. I don't want to come back and find you doing something stupid, Pa.'

'Take a look at the path of the fire,' Pete urged. 'We can't save the house but we could prevent the grass around this end of the creek burning. Let's get over there and start beating, or there'll be nothing left between here and Pine Flats.'

Clay saw at a glance that Pete was

right and swerved his horse to head through the smoke towards the creek. Pete followed him and they tied their horses to a tree that was out of the path of the fire and hurried into the water. Clay stripped off his shirt, soaked it, and began to beat at the flames trying to get around the end of the creek. He was half blinded and choked by the swiftly drifting smoke.

They fought what seemed to be a losing battle against the fire, but stayed at their task until the fight turned in their favour. Eventually, Clay straightened his aching back and looked at his father. Pete was breathless, and dropped to the ground, coughing hoarsely, his face blackened.

'Looks like we got it beat, Clay,' he observed. 'But just what the hell is going on? Yesterday the stream was blocked, and now the ranch is burned down. I reckon that prisoner you brought in has got a lot of questions to answer. I took his horse, so if he's bolted he won't be able to get far. Go round him up, Clay, and we'll talk to him.'

'I reckon you better head for town right now,' Clay advised. 'You can't do any good around here, and it might not be safe to stick around on your own. I'll pick up Shorty, bring him to town, and see you there.'

'I'll leave right away.' Pete nodded. 'Be careful picking up that hardcase. I'll be waiting for you in Pine Flats.'

Clay pushed himself wearily to his feet. He looked towards the house and saw only a heap of smoking ruins. A thread of anger burned in his chest and he sighed heavily. He was sweating and dirty, smoke-blackened, and pulled on his wet shirt, which was burned and scorched in places. He went to his horse and swung into the saddle to ride back into the yard. The pall of smoke had lessened and he looked around, checking the dust for boot prints. He found where Shorty had set out away from the spread and rode fast to catch the man.

It did not take him long to spot a

man's figure ahead, and Shorty glanced over his shoulder and halted when he saw Clay's grim figure bearing down upon him. He lifted his hands in token of surrender and sat down on the ground. Clay rode up to him and stepped down from his saddle.

'Say, I'm real sorry your house burned down,' Shorty said quickly, 'and I sure hope you don't think I know anything about it. I blocked your stream, sure, but I wouldn't stoop so low as to burn a man out of house and home.'

'I don't believe you.' Clay gritted teeth as he clenched his left hand into a fist and slammed hard knuckles against Shorty's jaw. 'You better come up with some straight answers pretty quick or there won't be much left of you by the time you hit jail in Pine Flats.'

Shorty picked himself up, spread his hands and shrugged. 'What can I tell you?' he asked. 'I'll give you what I know if you'll stop the rough stuff.'

'You've got a deal. Where did those

two pards of yours head for when they pulled out from the dam with the wagon? A shack was mentioned. Where is that?'

Shorty shook his head in resignation. 'It's a line shack on the edge of the Truscott ranch,' he said reluctantly. 'We got permission to stop over there for a spell.'

'Who gave you permission? Was it someone who rides for FT?'

'I don't know who he is. My two pards got the job down here. We were up around Dodge City a few weeks ago and Toomey, one of the guys with the wagon, met a man he had worked with before and was offered work down in this neck of the woods. We had nothing better to do so we rode south and started in. That dam was the first thing we did.'

'What's the name of the man who offered you the job?' Clay insisted.

Shorty shook his head. 'I never even saw him. Rafe Toomey told me about the deal and I threw in with him and

Sim Martin. They handled all the details.'

'And came along here after leaving the dam to fire our range,' Clay observed.

'I never heard it mentioned that your place would be torched. I tell you, mister, I wouldn't have had any part of burning you out.'

'But you're on your way back to that line shack to take part in whatever else is being planned, huh? Well, I got news for you. I'll turn you loose here and now and you'd better be long gone from this range by sundown, because if I set eyes on you again I'll gutshoot you. And that's a promise, not a threat. Do I make myself clear? Get off this range and don't come back.'

'I'll do that, mister! I don't want any part of this trouble now I know what is involved. I'll get out and keep going.'

'Then start right now, and don't head for that line shack on FT.'

'Which direction is that town you mentioned?'

'Head south and keep going. I don't want to set eyes on you again.'

Shorty nodded and turned south. He almost ran as he departed, and Clay stood watching him until he had disappeared over a crest before swinging into his saddle and riding on. His thoughts moved quickly as he considered what he had been told. Someone had deliberately brought trouble on to the range — someone on the FT ranch.

Clay wondered about the mystery man who had allegedly hired the three hardcases. He rode towards the spot where the fire had started but found nothing significant, and was aware that it was all too easy to start a range fire in these parts in high summer — a carelessly thrown match was all it took. He turned his gaze to the west, where the FT ranch was situated, and sent his sorrel in that direction. If Toomey and Martin were still at that line shack then he wanted an accounting with them.

Shadows were long on the range now, and Clay judged that it would be dark long before he reached the line shack. The sun went down behind a distant ridge and full dark covered the land but he kept riding. It was around midnight when he drew near to the line shack. He dismounted way out of hearing and made camp, ate cold food before turning into his blanket, and quickly fell asleep despite the problems on his mind. He slept peacefully until the first rays of the rising sun touched his face.

Clay left his horse in cover and walked to the shack, circling to approach it from the rear. There were two horses in a small corral behind the shack, and Clay recognized them as having been tied behind the wagon at the dam. He found cover close by and waited patiently for the occupants of the shack to show themselves. An hour passed before one of the two men he had seen at the dam came out to take care of the horses. He saw smoke begin to pour out of the small chimney on the roof of the shack and guessed the other man was cooking breakfast.

The man tending the horses was tall and thin, and wore a pistol low-slung on his right thigh; his hand never strayed far from the weapon. He fetched water in a bucket from a nearby water-hole and filled a small trough just inside the corral before lugging a small sack from the wagon parked under an adjacent tree and spilling a quantity of crushed oats on the grass. Clay watched intently, waiting for the man to finish his chores and return to the shack. When the man finally started back, Clay eased out of cover to follow, his gun in his hand.

But, as he reached the rear corner of the shack he heard the thud of approaching hoofs somewhere out front, and flattened himself against the rough woodwork of the shack. He heard voices, and craned forward to risk a peek along the side of the building. A man on a grey horse was cantering towards the shack, and called loudly to herald his approach.

Clay squinted through the early morning sunlight for a good look at the newcomer, and shock spilled through him when he recognized Mike Cade. Although he hadn't seen Cade in several years he had good cause to remember him, a nephew of Thurlow Payne, the foreman of the FT ranch. Cade had once spent a year at FT and made himself a nuisance to everyone. He had tried to ingratiate himself into Sue's favour, and became such a pest that Clay had given him the thrashing of his life. Cade had returned to where he came from and Clay had not expected him to show up ever again. But here he was in the flesh, and he seemed to be on friendly terms with the two hardcases.

Clay remained in cover at the back of the shack. Cade dismounted out front, and voices sounded until he entered the shack. Clay moved around to the opposite front corner and remained in concealment. He would dearly have liked to eavesdrop on the conversation taking place in the shack, but had no wish to reveal his presence. He waited patiently until Cade took his leave.

Mike Cade was in his early twenties, a powerfully built man with muscular arms. He was tall and handsome, with an arrogant swing to his broad shoulders that touched a chord in Clay's mind and reminded him of all the bad things Cade had done in the past. Cade swung into his saddle with easy grace and turned the grey to look down at the two men who had emerged from the shack to see him off.

'So you've got it straight, huh?' Cade asked. 'With the Bar O ranch house burned, Clay Overman and his old man will head for town to make a complaint to the law. You two get along to Pine Flats and put them both out of circulation.'

'Kill them, you mean?' said one of the two men.

'I don't want you to play games with them,' Cade said smoothly. 'The sooner you put Clay Overman down the better. Head for town as soon as you've eaten, and when you've handled the chore you

34

can come to FT. I'll be waiting there for you.'

'What about the local law?' the other hardcase demanded. 'We could be in trouble if we shoot someone inside of town limits.'

'There's a deputy by the name of Snape Ritter, and you don't have to worry about him,' Cade replied with a grin. 'I sounded him out last week and he'll turn a blind eye to anything that happens to Bar O.'

Clay clenched his teeth, aware that he needed no further proof of Cade's trouble-making. He lifted his hand to the butt of his pistol but stayed the movement, aware that he would be taking on more than he could handle by bracing three men out here in the wilderness. Cade was the man he really wanted, and he watched as Cade turned his grey and rode off in the direction of FT. When the two hard-cases went back into the shack, Clay sneaked away to get his horse.

He saddled the sorrel and rode out

after Cade, riding wide around the line shack and, when he saw Cade ahead, slowed his pace so as not to alert the man to the fact that he was being tailed. He considered the situation as he rode, wondering exactly how he should handle the problem. If Ritter was prepared to work with Cade then it would be useless trying to get help from that quarter. He hoped his father had not fallen foul of Ritter when he had ridden into town the night before.

It was at this time when Clay sensed that he was being followed, and he rode into cover, fearing that the two men back at the line shack had somehow become aware of his presence. He dismounted, led the sorrel into a weed-choked gully, and tethered it before taking his Winchester and back-tracking some twenty yards to lie in wait watching his trail. Sweat beaded his forehead as he tried to relax, but he was disturbed by what he had learned about Cade and was filled with concern.

When a rider appeared on a crest some fifty yards back Clay frowned, for he recognized Snape Ritter instantly. The deputy sheriff was mounted on a powerful chestnut stallion. Clay watched Ritter come off the crest, head bent to one side as he looked intently for hoofprints. Clay set his teeth into his bottom lip. Ritter was tracking him. He waited until the deputy drew level with his position and then stood up quickly, covering Ritter with the rifle.

'You're trailing me, Ritter,' he challenged.

Snape Ritter reined in, a big man, his fleshy figure heavy and well-muscled. His face was large and rounded, his brown eyes small, like a hog's, and his mouth was just a mean slit under his prominent nose. He gazed down at Clay, his eyes narrowed to the merest slits under the wide brim of his black Stetson, and a tight grin stretched his fleshy lips.

'Well, look who's popped up outa the

brush!' he declared. 'You're a damn sidewinder! You've covered a lot of range since last night, Overman. I arrested your old man in town when he showed up and he gave me some cock and bull story about the Bar O ranch house being burned down. He said you were out here looking for three hardcases causing you trouble, so I came out after you.'

'Did you come by the FT line shack back there?' Clay demanded.

'I sure did, and found two FT punchers watching the stock in that area. They didn't know you'd been around there until I showed them your tracks. So why are you sneaking around? What are you up to, trailing in this direction?'

'I'm on the trail of Mike Cade, who was at the line shack at sunup this morning, giving orders to murder me and my pa to the two hardcases hiding out there.'

'Who is Mike Cade?' Ritter was inching his right hand towards the butt of his holstered pistol. 'I've never heard of him.'

'That's strange, considering you threw in your lot with him last week. He's a nephew of Thurlow Payne, and you know who Payne is, huh?'

'Sure. Payne is foreman at FT. You better put that rifle away, or you'll find yourself under arrest for threatening a lawman. I'm gonna take you to town and jail you along with your old man.'

'Just try it,' Clay retorted. 'I'd like an excuse to gutshoot you.'

'OK. You've got the drop on me so what's your next move? You ain't got a leg to stand on unless you shoot me in cold blood. Is that what you've got in mind?'

'Why did you arrest my pa? If you've harmed him in any way you'll be real sorry.'

'Do you reckon you can take me?' Ritter's eyes gleamed like polished pebbles. 'I'd sure like you to put down that rifle and get your fists up like a man. I didn't hurt your pa real bad;

only roughed him up a little. So why don't you try and get some of your own back, huh?'

'Get rid of your pistol,' Clay rasped, 'and don't try any fool play when you do it. Use your finger and thumb only. I'd just like for you to try something. Come on, get moving. Throw down your gun and then climb out of leather.'

Ritter made a great show of lifting his pistol with finger and thumb, and froze the movement for a couple of seconds before dropping the weapon into the dust. Then he dismounted and, as his feet touched the ground, he hurled himself at Clay with the speed and power of a mountain lion. His big hands lifted to grab at Clay's rifle and a reckless laugh spilled through his thick lips.

Clay was half-expecting such a move and was poised for it. He sidestepped Ritter's lunge, swung his rifle in a vicious arc, and smashed the butt into Ritter's face. Ritter swung away with a shout of pain and plunged face down into the dust. Clay covered him with the rifle, his features set in a mask of fury.

'If you've hurt my pa I'll tear you apart, Ritter,' he rasped. 'You're a poor excuse for a deputy. You've been riding roughshod around the county far too long, and it's about time you were pulled up sharp. I'm riding into FT before I go on to town, and when I reach Pine Flats I'll spread the word about you. The sheriff will be mighty interested in what you're doing. Now you'd better get out of here, and stay out of my way or I'll kill you. You've set upon the wrong man with your trouble-making, and I'll see the whole bunch of you in Hell before I'm through.'

Clay reached out with his left hand and removed the Winchester rifle nestling in the saddle boot on Ritter's horse. He stepped back, covering the lawman, and watched Ritter sit up, his hands to his face and blood trickling through his splayed fingers.

'Go on, get on your hind legs and move out,' Clay rasped. 'If you've got any sense you'll head for other parts. You're finished around here. If I set eyes on you again I'll put a slug in your brisket. Get to hell out before I change my mind and shoot you right now.'

Ritter pushed himself to his feet and stood swaying, his left hand holding his face where the rifle butt had struck him. He spat blood, and then reached into his mouth with finger and thumb, located a loose tooth, and jerked it out. He gazed at the tooth for a moment before putting it into a breast pocket of his leather vest.

'You're gonna be a mighty sorry man when I meet up with you again,' he promised, wiping blood from his lips with the back of his left hand. 'Your days are numbered now. I won't need paying for putting you down in the dust; I'll do it for free. You can try to run but it won't do you any good. I'll hunt you down and finish you off before I kill your old man.'

'Talk is cheap,' Clay retorted. 'Get up on that horse and pull out. I've got your measure, Ritter.'

The deputy scowled and climbed into his saddle. He reined the horse around to gaze down at Clay, and there was a murderous gleam in his dark eyes. Clay kept him covered with his Winchester. Ritter spat blood again and then wheeled his horse and set spurs into its flanks. He rode back the way he had come, and Clay remained motionless until the deputy had passed out of sight.

Clay stuffed Ritter's pistol into his waistband and thrust the deputy's Winchester under the straps of one of his saddle-bags. He rode on to the FT ranch, watching Cade's tracks in the dust, and when he came in sight of the ranch and saw Big Frank Truscott standing by the corral at the back of the yard, talking to Mike Cade, he drew a long, steadying breath before riding in to confront the two men . . .

3

'You've got a nerve, Clay,' Big Frank said stridently as Clay reined up in front of him. 'I lost some steers last night from the home pasture, and my night hawk gave me a description of one of the rustlers which fitted you like a Sunday suit. So what have you got to say for yourself?'

Clay gazed at Sue's father and all his old dislike for the man's ability to pick at weakness in a lesser man, with words that ripped and tore like the beak of an eagle, rose in his mind. He knew only too well Frank's bantering way and odd sense of humour, but had always felt strangely defenceless against it. He looked into the rancher's fleshy, grinning face and wondered just what made the man tick, and in his present state of mind he wondered how Frank would face up to a punch on the jaw. In the middle fifties, Big Frank Truscott still retained the youthfulness of someone half his age. He was larger than life — built like a barn, and viewed life with a perpetual grin on his face, as if he found his progress through the years as one big joke.

'Say, you look like you just picked up a plugged nickel in your change from Wymer's store,' Frank continued. 'You wanta lighten up, Clay, because it may never happen.'

'It has happened,' Clay responded. 'Our stream was dammed last night this side of Water Canyon, and after I cleared the blockage someone set fire to the range upwind of Bar O and burned the ranch house.'

'The hell you say!' For once in his life Big Frank's casual manner vanished. He glanced quickly at Mike Cade, leaning casually against a corral post, and a shadow filled his eyes. 'I'm real sorry to hear that, Clay. Did you catch the men responsible?'

Clay shook his head. 'There was a lot

of sign on the range but no one to pin the blame on.'

'You've been out riding, Mike.' Frank turned to Cade. 'Did you see anything suspicious out there?'

'Not a thing!' Cade shook his head. 'But I wasn't riding in the direction of Bar O.'

'Do you remember Mike, Clay?' Frank asked. 'Payne's nephew from Montana; spent a lot of time here some years ago.'

'Mike Cade!' Clay nodded. It was in him to confront Cade with what he had learned, but decided to keep silent until he had figured the full extent of Cade's duplicity. He glanced at Cade and kept his tone neutral when he spoke. 'How could I ever forget you, Cade? You caused more trouble around here than a wagonload of monkeys. I never met a youngster who could upset so many folks without really trying.'

'I was just naturally high-spirited.' Cade smiled broadly but his gaze did not lose its harsh glitter. 'There was nothing bad in what I pulled back in those days. I do remember that you gave me one helluva beating when you couldn't take any more, but I've grown up some since then. Now butter wouldn't melt in my mouth.'

Clay studied Cade's smooth face, keenly aware that he was lying through his teeth. Cade had grown into a big frame with well-developed muscles. His brown eyes held a gleam as if a devil still possessed him. He was dressed in good range clothes and carried a .45 pistol in a low slung holster on his right thigh. The grin on his fleshy lips was the same as it had been years ago — tormenting, cynical, and always present while his tricky brain planned mischief; only now the mischief was no longer boyish.

'I'll bet Sue wasn't pleased to see you again,' Clay opined.

'I've apologized to her for my behaviour all those years ago, and I hope we can bury the hatchet, Clay.' Cade held out his hand, his smile enigmatic.

'Like you said, it was mainly boyish stuff.' Clay touched Cade's hand briefly, but anger filled him when he considered Cade's involvement with Shorty and his two pards. He would just have to watch this newcomer like a hawk, and drop on to him at the first real proof of culpability.

'Is there anything I can do to help, Clay?' Big Frank asked. 'I'll send Will Hardy and some of the crew over to Bar O tomorrow and they can start rebuilding.'

'That's real good of you but hold your fire on that until we get who is responsible. If we don't catch them they'll only continue the trouble.'

'Have you informed the law yet?' Big Frank persisted.

Clay grimaced. 'Pete went into town to set the wheels in motion, although I don't expect any help from that direction. You know what Ritter is like.'

'You'd do better by going straight to Sheriff Cooper in Sunset Ridge,' Big Frank observed. 'Why don't you do that? And take Will Brennan and Jake Barlow along with you. They are pretty handy with a gun. I'll do all I can to help, Clay. We ranchers have got to stick together when this kind of trouble strikes.'

'I'll let you know if I need any help,' Clay responded.

'Is there any particular reason why you rode in here?' Cade asked. His eyes were filled with a piercing brightness as he held Clay's gaze, as if challenging Clay to reveal what he knew, if anything. 'Shouldn't you be out looking for your enemies?'

'I am looking for them.' Clay nodded. 'I rode this way to warn you, Frank, to be on your guard. There's no telling when those hellions will strike again or who will be their next target.'

'I'd welcome the chance to meet some trouble-makers.' Big Frank stuck out his prominent chin. 'I guess I'll have to start riding the range again. Since I've been sticking close to home the bad men have got bolder.'

'No one in his right mind would deliberately pick on you,' Clay observed. 'You're too big. It's Bar O they've hit.'

'The least I can do is put some of my crew to riding your range,' Big Frank insisted. 'They'll soon get the measure of your trouble and kill it dead.'

'I've got a feeling it won't be that easy,' Clay retorted.

'Hi there, stranger, I don't expect you've come to see me, have you?' Sue Truscott's voice rang musically from behind Clay and he turned quickly to look at the girl, experiencing a rush of unaccustomed emotion as he looked at her lovely face.

'Hi, Sue,' he replied. 'Long time no see!'

'You do know where to find me,' she challenged, her blue eyes narrowed.

'It's my fault entirely.' Clay grimaced. 'I guess I've been neglecting my friends lately.' He drew a deep breath as he ran his gaze over her lithe figure. She was a pretty girl, with blonde hair that was tied back in a pony-tail. She was wearing Levi's and a blouse, and a flat-crowned plains hat to keep the sun off her face. She looked tanned and healthy, but her eyes carried shadows in them, and he did not have to ask why.

'You don't look so good,' she remarked. 'What have you been up to? Is that smoke I can smell on you?'

'Someone burned down the Bar O ranch house,' Frank said. 'Clay was just telling us about it.'

'I was shot at from cover last week,' Clay added, 'and the slug didn't miss me by a mile.' He was watching Mike Cade as he spoke, and saw Cade's lips compress against his teeth. He would have given a lot to know what was passing through the man's mind and had to fight against the impulse to call Cade out, his fingers tingling at the thought.

'Come and walk with me,' Sue invited. 'Now you're here I'd better take advantage of the fact. You used to be a regular visitor, but times have certainly changed. Now I only see you once in a blue moon. Bring your horse over to the barn.'

Clay opened his mouth to protest that he was too busy but Sue's level gaze held much that warned him she had something on her mind. He led the sorrel across the yard, only half listening to Sue's chatter. She slipped an arm through his and clung to him tightly until they were out of earshot of her father and Mike Cade.

'I'm so glad you've showed up at last,' she said, her tone altering. 'I'm feeling so desperate about the situation here that I almost rode over to your place to see you.'

'You've got a problem?' Clay demanded.

'Mike Cade is a problem wherever he's at,' Sue responded. 'Surely you haven't forgotten what he was like as a boy!'

'That was kid's stuff. He must have changed some over the years.'

'He's changed all right, and not for the better. I didn't like him as a boy — now I can't stand the sight of him, and it looks like he's here to stay. He's moved in with Payne and talks of putting down roots.'

'What brought him here?'

'His father died a couple of months ago and he decided to spend some time with his only living relative, poor Payne, who was embarrassed by Cade's arrival and apologized to Big Frank, but you know what Pa is like. He said Cade can stay as long as he likes, and can have a job here if he needs one.'

'And you don't like it,' Clay observed.

'Are you kidding? You know what I thought of Mike Cade when he was here before. That was bad enough, but now he is full grown he is worse than I could ever have imagined. He's only been here a couple of weeks but already he's hinting about marrying me! I can't move around the place without falling over him. I haven't known a moment's peace since his arrival, and no matter what I say to Big Frank he just won't take me seriously.'

Clay suppressed a sigh. It was on the

tip of his tongue to tell Sue what he had learned about Cade but remained silent. There was time enough to spill the beans when he had gathered more evidence of Cade's involvement in the trouble that had struck Bar O.

'I want you to help me out, Clay.' Sue paused in the doorway of the barn and turned to face him. Her expression showed deep concern and he realized just how worried she was.

'Sure,' he replied. 'Anything you say. If you want me to give Cade another beating I'll oblige. It's obvious that first beating hasn't taught him anything.'

'I want you to pretend that we've got something going between us.' Sue grasped his arm tightly. 'Please, Clay, I'm really worried about the way Cade is acting. If I don't put my foot down right now there'll be no stopping him. I've heard Payne talking to him, telling him to put on the brakes, but Cade never listened to anyone in his life, and he's got plans to marry me, no matter what I say. He's like a runaway train.

Nothing will stop him.'

Clay shook his head as he glanced back at the yard. Cade was watching them. Clay recalled the scene he had witnessed at the line shack and Cade's words were repeated in his mind. He had all the evidence he needed right now to set Cade back on his heels, but was aware that it would be his word against Cade's and that was not enough to pin the responsibility where it belonged.

'Are you taking in what I'm saying?' Sue demanded. 'It's getting real bad around here. I'm thinking of moving into town while Cade is here just to get away from him. I could stay with Aggie Spooner, but it goes deeper than that. I daren't leave Big Frank here because I think Cade has ulterior motives. I've seen his expression during unguarded moments, and I fear something will happen to my father if I'm not here to watch his back.'

'Are you serious?' Clay frowned. He looked intently into Sue's eyes and gauged the intensity of her feelings. 'Say, you are feeling bad,' he observed.

He nodded. 'Sure, I'll go along with what you suggest if you need my backing. So you and I have an understanding, huh? Are we talking wedding bells here?'

'I think we can hint that we have a mind to settle down together; that should be enough to keep Cade off my neck.'

'And if it doesn't then I'll put it to him more forcefully. Listen, Sue, I was gonna keep this to myself but in view of your feelings I think you should know what I've discovered.' He went on to explain the trouble he had experienced in the past hours and saw horror seep into Sue's expression.

'I don't know what to say,' Sue gasped. 'I've had suspicions, and what you've said bears out what I've felt. Do you know that Payne owns a quarter share of FT? He's been here with Big Frank ever since the ranch was founded, and put some money towards the first herd that was bought. I've been wondering what attracted Cade here in the first place, and it must be that. No doubt he's expecting to inherit Payne's share of the ranch.'

'But Payne ain't likely to die yet! He's got a lot more years in him.'

'Well, think about it,' Sue said harshly. 'I'm afraid, Clay. Trouble is breaking out on the range and it looks like it started after Cade arrived.'

Clay nodded. 'OK, you hold your horses right there. I'll go and throw a scare into Cade and we'll see which way he jumps.'

'What are you going to do?' Sue demanded in sudden alarm. 'You've got to take it easy, or you'll never get the proof you need.'

'I know what I'm doing,' Clay responded. He handed the sorrel's reins to Sue. 'Stay here and watch. I'll level with Cade so he'll know where he stands, and then if he steps out of line any place I'll be able to take him.'

'Be careful, Clay,' Sue warned. 'He

carries that big pistol on his hip but he's got a smaller hideout gun which he favours. I've seen him practising drawing it when he's been alone. It's in the right-hand pocket of his jacket.'

'It won't come to gunplay,' Clay said confidently, and turned on his heel and walked back across the yard to the corral.

Big Frank was on his way back to the house when Clay reached the corral and Cade was falling into step beside the rancher.

'Do you want to talk to me, Clay?' Big Frank asked.

'No. I want a few words with Cade,' Clay replied, pausing in front of Cade.

'What can I do for you?' Cade demanded.

Big Frank walked on and Clay waited until the rancher was out of earshot. Cade watched Clay intently, a derisive smile on his lips.

'So what's on your mind, Clay?' Cade asked.

'Just a little straight talking,' Clay

shrugged his wide shoulders and his voice took on a harsh note. 'We need to clear the air about Sue. She's my girl and we plan to marry one day so turn your attention elsewhere. I want to keep this friendly, but if you step out of line where Sue is concerned I'll drop on to you and squash you flat. Do you get my drift?'

'Hey, there's no need to come the hard man with me, Clay. I'm merely being friendly. Sue and me — we go back a long way.'

'I know. I was around the last time you were here and I had to straighten you out then, but it looks like you've forgotten about that.'

Cade shook his head, his eyes suddenly filled with a dull gleam. 'I haven't forgotten anything,' he said sharply. 'You reckon you're a big man, Clay, but you can be cut down to size.'

'If you fancy trying it then let's step into the barn and get to it,' Clay responded eagerly. 'You're getting in Sue's hair, and I'm the one she turns to for help. I'm trying to keep this friendly, but I don't think you have the sense to face up to the facts, so if I've got to teach you another lesson then I'm ready, willing and able.'

Cade lifted his right hand to his jacket pocket and reached inside. Clay waited until the hand began to reappear, and when he caught the glint of metal in Cade's fist he reached out with his left hand and grasped Cade's wrist, staying the movement. He slid his right foot forward six inches and let his weight shift across to his right leg as his right hand whipped up and swung in a tight arc. His clenched fist slammed against Cade's jaw.

The smack of the blow sounded across the yard, and was followed by a cry from Cade, whose knees buckled. Clay dragged Cade's right hand out of the jacket pocket and tore a small pistol from the man's grasp. He flung the weapon away and hit Cade a second time, releasing his grip on Cade's arm as he crumpled into the dust.

Cade lay motionless on his back, his eyes closed, chest rising and falling quickly. Clay glanced around to see Big Frank gazing back to see what the disturbance was, his face showing shock. Sue was frozen in the background, gripping the sorrel's reins, her expression showing the extent of her concern.

Clay caught a movement out of the corner of his eye and turned his head to see Thurlow Payne coming around the corral at a run. The foreman's big figure was moving fast, his boots throwing up small puffs of dust as he planted them heavily on the hard ground. Clay glanced down at Cade, saw that he was senseless, and stepped back to prepare to face Payne in the event the foreman might want to take Cade's part.

'What in hell is going on here?' Payne demanded, as he dropped to one knee beside Cade. 'I thought that trouble between you and Mike was boy's stuff. I saw you ride in, Clay. So what brought this on? You're getting too fond

61

of throwing your weight around.'

'It's not my play, Thurlow,' Clay replied as the foreman regained his feet. He pointed to where the hideout gun was lying in the dust. 'I was just giving Cade some friendly rules to live by around here and he reckoned to use that. I didn't wait for him to start shooting because it seemed easier to disarm him and find out afterwards what is on his mind.'

Big Frank came back to them, his large face set in a forbidding frown. He pushed the foreman back on his heels and confronted Clay.

'Stay outa this, Thurlow,' Frank growled. 'This is between two young men, and if you try to smooth it over now it will only bust out again later. Clay, I don't like you roughing up a man who is my guest. I know you're under a lot of pressure right now, but that don't excuse your behaviour. Get out of here before Cade gets on his feet. I don't want gunplay in my front yard so mount up and split the breeze.'

'Hold your horses, Pa!' Sue approached leading Clay's sorrel. Her face was pale and her expression showed fear. 'Don't go off half-cocked! Clay was having a word with Cade because I asked him to. I saw Cade reach for his gun before Clay made a move. If anyone should be shown the door it is Cade. Give him his marching orders, or I'll be forced to leave. I'm sick of being hounded in my own home. Cade is intolerable.'

'Has Cade been bothering you? Heck, why didn't you speak up before this?' Big Frank's expression changed. 'You didn't have to get Clay to stand up for you. What kind of a father do you think I am? Just wait until I've taken Cade in hand.'

'I didn't want to cause any trouble,' Sue said heavily. 'I thought if Clay had a word in Cade's ear the matter would be resolved. But Cade must have taken it the wrong way.'

Cade was beginning to stir. His eyes flickered open. He lifted his head to look around, and surprise showed in his face when he found himself lying flat on his back in the dust. His gaze went to where Clay was standing and his right hand lifted to his vest pocket, found his hideout gun was missing, and then dropped to the .45 nestling in his holster.

Payne stepped forward a short pace and bent to snatch the pistol from Cade's holster.

'Leave it be, Mike,' the foreman warned harshly. 'You've already made a fool of yourself so don't add to it. Get up and go to my shack. We'll have words later. I warned you to behave yourself around here and you've let me down. I am not pleased, and you'll answer to me for what has happened.'

Payne's gaze lifted to Big Frank, who nodded.

'I'll leave it in your hands, Thurlow,' Frank decided. 'You deal with it. If Cade has been harassing Sue then he's gonna be out of here before sundown. Is that clear? My daughter comes first in everything. If she isn't happy with

Cade around, then he goes.'

'Sure, Frank. I'll handle it.' Payne reached down, grasped Cade's left arm and dragged him to his feet. 'I don't know what's been going on, but Mike is under a lot of strain right now, what with his father's death. I'll set him straight, don't you fear.'

Clay heaved a long sigh as Payne led Cade away. Sue came to his side and slipped an arm through his. Clay glanced at her as she spoke to her father.

'You haven't heard all of it yet, Pa,' Sue said. 'Clay and I have an understanding. It's early days yet, but we intend to marry in the future.'

Clay watched Big Frank's face, saw the rancher's expression change yet again, and sensed that the news was not well received. He clenched his teeth and awaited the inevitable demoralizing banter that Frank generally used to cover his real thoughts.

'Is that a fact?' Frank demanded. A smile appeared on his lips and he nodded. 'You look mighty serious, Sue. How do you feel about it, Clay? You ain't looking too pleased. Is Sue twisting your arm over this? I know a gal worth her salt can twist any man around her little finger. If you feel any reluctance then now is the time to speak up and I'll put my foot down. Sue can have anything and do anything as far as I'm concerned — I'd rope the moon for her if she wanted it — but I draw the line at her dragging someone into the family if he ain't one hundred per cent sure of his feelings.'

'I'm not hog-tied,' Clay replied. 'I feel the same way about Sue as you do, and if she's got marriage on her mind then that's OK by me.'

Big Frank nodded. 'You better come into the house and we'll have a drink on your decision,' he invited. 'Truth to tell, I have been wondering about you two. I've seen how Sue feels about you, but you always looked reluctant to go along with her wishes, Clay, and I've suspected that I've been putting you off. I do have an unfortunate manner, I know, but I'll go along with anything Sue wants. Is that clear?'

'Sure!' Clay smiled. He looked at Sue, noted her relief at the turn of events, and pushed his own worries into the background of his mind. 'But I'd better pull out now. Pa went into town yesterday while I rode along here, and I want to be on hand when he talks to the law about our trouble. I think he might find more to handle in town than he expects. I'll come back to see you tomorrow, Sue.'

'I'll be waiting for you,' she replied eagerly.

Clay nodded, and suppressed a sigh as he swung into his saddle and prepared to ride out.

4

Clay was relieved when he left the FT ranch. He followed the well-defined trail that led to Pine Flats and pushed the sorrel along at a fast clip, his thoughts moving quickly. He needed to talk to his father, and wondered how Pete would react when he learned about Mike Cade's involvement in the trouble that had developed. Knowing his father as he did, he suspected that a big confrontation would take place, and he was worried by the prospect of having to use his gun, even in self-defence.

Pine Flats was an untidy straggle of buildings along the trail through a valley that curved across the range from north to south. Water glinted in a shallow river that followed the line of the valley and which had its source in the distant mountains. It was well past noon when Clay sighted the little town, and he skirted a corral and rode into the livery barn on his left. He stepped down from his saddle as Walt Massey, the liveryman, appeared from his office and came forward. Massey was tall and thin, his angular cheeks covered with straggly grey hair that was badly in need of a trim. His mouth was concealed by his unruly beard and his long thin nose poked towards Clay like an accusing finger. His narrowed brown eyes glinted from deep sockets.

'Say, you sure took your time to show up, Clay,' Massey growled. 'I sent word to you last night about your Pa, saying it was urgent.'

'What about Pete?' Clay demanded. He reached out a big hand and grasped Massey's arm. 'Has something happened to him?'

'He came into town late and was in a helluva mood. I heard shouting on the street and went out to see what was going on. Pete was standing up to Snape Ritter and giving that no-good deputy hell about something that had happened on the range. Ritter didn't like being told he was a poor excuse for a lawman and arrested Pete. That's when I sent Billy Turrell to warn you what had happened.'

'I wasn't at the ranch,' Clay responded. 'Is my pa still in the jail?'

'Yeah, as far as I know. I'll take care of your horse while you slip along there and try to sort out the trouble. Pete was madder than a wet hen, and he wouldn't apologize to Ritter. I heard later that your ranch house was burned down yesterday. Is that the truth, Clay?'

'It burned down,' Clay replied harshly. He turned on his heel, left the barn, and hurried along the street.

A voice called his name from the doorway of Bennett's saloon and he lifted a hand in acknowledgement but kept on to the law office. He was breathing hard when he tried the door of the office and found it locked. He glanced around the street, and then walked to the doorway of the nearby gun shop. Amos Berry, the gunsmith, looked up when Clay entered the shop, and reached for a carton of .45 cartridges.

'How are you, Clay?' Berry demanded. He straightened his tall, lean figure and looked at Clay with questioning blue eyes. 'You will need these if you've come to bust Pete outa jail.'

'The law office is locked. I saw Ritter out by FT this morning. Is Edlin minding the office?'

'Yeah! He usually stands in for Ritter, and you'll find him in the saloon about this time. Do you want these shells?'

'Not right now.' Clay turned away, his right hand unconsciously brushing the flared handle of his holstered pistol.

His boots rapped the boardwalk as he strode back to the saloon, where he paused at the batwings and peered inside the gloomy building. Ray Warner, the bartender, was wiping down the polished bar top while chatting to three customers bellied up to the bar. Clay saw that one of the three was Paul

71

Edlin, the undertaker, and he shouldered through the swing doors and stalked across to the long counter, his heels thudding resolutely on the bare pine boards.

Voices fell silent when he was recognized. He paused beside Edlin, who raised a glass of beer to his lips and drank deeply before setting down the glass and wiping his mouth on a sleeve. Edlin smacked his lips and looked around.

'Damned sawdust gets lodged in the back of the throat,' Edlin declared. 'For years I told Martha it takes several drinks when I finish a coffin to clear the dust, but she didn't ever believe me. Howdy, Clay. You heard about Pete being locked in the jail?'

'I heard. Did Ritter show up in town this morning?'

'I don't give a damn where Ritter is.' Edlin picked up his glass again and Clay reached out and pressed a hand on the undertaker's wrist, forcing the glass back to the bar.

'Give me a minute of your time right now and you can spend the rest of the day drinking,' Clay said sharply. 'Where is Ritter?'

'How the hell should I know?' Edlin flared. 'I ain't Ritter's keeper!'

'What did he tell you about Pete?'

'He said to keep Pete behind bars until he gets back. You better back off, Clay! I got the power to arrest folks when Ritter is out of town. Pete asked for trouble, coming in last night to raise hell. He shouldn't have struck Ritter. That's why he's behind bars, and he'll have to stay there until he apologizes for making a fool of Ritter. You know that big baboon won't give an inch when it comes to his duty. What's wrong with your family anyway? Pete ain't one to raise a ruckus.'

'I want to see Pete now,' Clay said impatiently. 'It is important. Come and unlock the jail. I've had a tough day so don't run me ragged.'

'Not right now.' Edlin reached for his glass. 'I got a lot of dust in my throat.

Come back an hour from now and I'll let you see your pa.'

'I want to see him now, Edlin.' A harsh note crept into Clay's voice. 'Let's get moving. The sooner I see Pete the sooner you can get back to your beer.'

'Hold your horses!' Edlin's tone roughened. 'Where do you get off — coming in here and ordering me to do what you want? I've just finished a day's work and I need a few drinks. It was Pete's fault he got put behind bars, and he'll stay there no matter what you want.'

'Save your breath,' Clay rasped. 'And don't make trouble for yourself. I want to see Pete now and you're gonna open up the jail for me, so let's get moving.'

'The hell I will!' Edlin backed way from the bar, his face changing expression. 'Get the hell outa here, Clay, before you go the same way Pete did. What's got into you and your old man? Is there something in the water out at Bar O?'

Clay lost his patience and dropped a hand to his pistol. 'You better do like I say, or you'll find yourself up to your neck in something you can't handle,' he warned.

'You're threatening me!' Alarm showed on Edlin's face.

'Come on,' Clay urged. 'Let's get this done. I wanta see my pa right now.'

Edlin shrugged and exhaled in a long sigh. 'OK,' he said grudgingly. 'I'll go along with you, but I'll report this to Ritter when he gets back. You're piling up a load of trouble for yourself, Clay. You can't push the law around, not in this town you can't.'

Clay took Edlin by the arm and led him to the batwings. They departed and walked to the law office. Edlin complained incessantly, but he produced a bunch of keys, selected one, and unlocked the law office door.

'I can't turn Pete loose,' Edlin warned, as they entered.

'I'm not asking you to. Just give me five minutes to talk to him. I have a right to see him.'

Edlin paused on the threshold and held out the jail keys. 'Here, take them and do what you have to. But don't turn Pete loose, and bring the keys back to me when you've finished.'

Clay took the keys and Edlin departed quickly, leaving Clay staring after him. Clay shook his head, locked the street door, and then walked to the desk and picked up a bunch of cell keys. He unlocked the door between the office and the cells and walked into the cell block.

'I'm sure glad to see you, Clay,' Pete said. He was standing at the door of a locked cell, his hands gripping the bars. 'Where the hell have you been? I expected you to show up last night.'

'I'll tell you about it in a moment,' Clay responded. 'You'd better tell me what the hell you're doing in jail. Ain't we in enough trouble without you roughing up Ritter?'

'I didn't do anything,' Pete protested. 'Heck, you know I wouldn't step out of line where the law is concerned, even with a no-good deputy like Ritter. I came into town to make a report on what happened out at the ranch and met Ritter on the street near the livery barn. When I started in to tell him about our troubles he cut me short and said he didn't want to know because we were troublemakers, and anything that happened to us was our own fault.'

Clay's eyes glimmered with anger as he stared at his father.

'And that ain't all,' Pete continued. 'He started to push me around, and when I hit him he arrested me.'

'The hell you say!' Clay shook his head.

'I've had all night to think about it,' Pete said grimly, 'and the only answer I can come up with is that Ritter is mixed up in our trouble somewhere. Say, how did you manage to get in here? Where is Ritter? If he put me in jail for no reason then he'll do the same to you.'

'Just hold your horses, Pa. When I tell you what happened to me you'll mebbe get a better idea of what's going on.' Clay recounted his experiences since leaving the Bar O the day before.

Pete listened without interruption, his face set in a grave expression. He nodded when Clay had brought him up to date.

'So Mike Cade is behind it, huh?' he exclaimed. 'I remember that young 'un from ten years ago. He was a polecat then and he sounds like he ain't changed any over the years. He's Payne's nephew, so is Payne in this with him?'

'Your guess is as good as mine,' Clay responded 'But I do know Ritter has thrown in with Cade.' He recounted his meeting with the deputy. 'I don't like this at all, Pa, and I've got a feeling that you've got to get out of here before anything worse happens.'

Pete stared into Clay's eyes. 'Say, you don't think Ritter is planning to put me out of the way, huh?' he demanded.

'I wouldn't be surprised by anything right now,' Clay countered.

Pete nodded slowly. 'You better let me out of here and we'll hightail it out of town. We'll go to FT, grab Cade, and make him tell us what he's up to. You heard him talking to those two skunks at the line shack, and you know those two had something to do with the stream being dammed, along with that feller you brought to the ranch. As I see it, we've got plenty of evidence about what's going on, and if we grab Cade we can ride over to Sunset Ridge and dump him in the sheriff's lap.'

'Do you think we can trust Sheriff Cooper?' Clay demanded. 'After what's happened here, I don't know who to trust any more.'

'There's only one way we'll find out.' Pete shook the bars of the cell door. 'Let me out of here, Clay, and we'll put Bill Cooper to the test.'

Clay inserted a key in the cell door and turned it. Pete grasped the door, dragged it open, and sighed with relief as he stepped out of the cell. He froze when a noise sounded at the street door in the outer office.

'Someone's outside,' Pete said. 'It could be Ritter coming back.'

Clay turned swiftly, and drew his pistol as he went into the office. 'Keep quiet, Pa, and I'll check it out,' he said over his shoulder.

A hand was shaking the street door on the outside and Clay heard voices when he reached the door. He stood motionless, listening intently.

'What the hell!' someone outside exclaimed. 'There's got to be a jailer in there. Someone must be in the office.'

'Ritter said there would be no one around,' a second voice observed. 'Here, let me try.'

'It's locked, I tell you.'

The door shook again, and Clay moved to the window overlooking the street and risked a glance outside. He saw two horses standing at the hitch rail in front of the office, but could not see the two men standing at the door. He moved back to the door and remained motionless, his breathing restrained.

The door was shaken violently, and one of the two men outside uttered a warning.

'Take it easy, Rafe. We don't want to rouse the town.'

'Ritter said it would be easy — no hitches — just come into town, take the prisoner out and kill him. So what is going on? Why is the door locked? There ain't but one deputy in this burg, and he's hiding out of town until we've disposed of Pete Overman.'

Clay was horror-stricken by the cold-blooded words. Here was undeniable proof that Ritter was mixed up in the trouble that had descended on Bar O. And the two men outside the door were the ones Cade had spoken to at the FT line shack. He glanced over his shoulder to find Pete standing close behind him. Pete held up a warning finger when Clay opened his mouth to speak.

They waited, Clay grasping his pistol in a sweaty hand.

'Kick the damned door and break the

lock,' a voice said impatiently.

'Are you loco? What are you gonna say when the townsmen come running? We're supposed to be working under cover. I don't like this, Rafe. Something bad is going on. And where's Shorty got to?'

'Ritter said he ain't seen him around, so he can't be in jail. Step back and keep watch. I'm gonna put my foot into the door and break the damn lock. We've got to get a move on. The sooner we get back out of town the better.'

Clay glanced at his father to see him moving back across the office. A gunbelt was hanging from a nail in the wall behind the desk. Pete buckled the belt around his waist and drew the pistol to check it. He eased the weapon back into the holster and returned to Clay's side, his face set in harsh lines, his pale eyes gleaming with determination.

'We've heard enough to be able to take action against those two out there, Clay,' Pete said in a hoarse whisper.

'You stand ready with your gun and I'll unlock the door and jerk it open. We should catch them cold. We'll take them prisoner.'

Clay drew a deep breath before nodding. He inserted a key in the lock, moved aside, and lifted his pistol. Pete drew his gun, held it ready, and reached out with his left hand to turn the key in the lock. He glanced at Clay to check that he was ready before jerking the door open.

One of the two men was standing on one leg in the act of kicking the door. He lost his balance when he failed to make contact and blundered forward into the doorway, falling to his hands and knees on the threshold of the office. Clay leaned forward and slammed the barrel of his pistol against the back of the man's neck He straightened quickly and levelled the weapon at the second man, who was standing a couple of feet back on the sidewalk, his hands empty and his face showing complete surprise.

Clay recognized the men as Toomey

and Martin from the FT line shack. He motioned with his gun and the man outside lifted his hands shoulder high and stepped forward into the office.

'What's your name, mister?' Clay demanded. 'Are you Toomey or Martin?'

'You know our names?' the man countered in surprise.

'I know a lot about you.' Clay reached out with his left hand and took the man's pistol from its holster. He relocked the street door. 'I saw you two at the dam with Shorty Allen, and trailed you to the line shack on the FT ranch. I watched Mike Cade visiting you there and heard what was said. So give me your name and then we'll get down to the business of finding out just what you are up to on our range.'

'I'm Sim Martin. That's Rafe Toomey on the floor. You were out at the line shack this morning, Ritter showed us your tracks. So where is he?'

'I'll ask the questions,' Clay said sharply. 'We heard you talking outside the door so we know what's going on.

You better give it to me straight, Martin.'

'Let's lock them in the cells,' Pete suggested. 'They are gonna have to get used to being cooped up. They were gonna take me out of town and kill me. Well, it's OK if they want to play it like that. We'll handle them as they would have treated me.'

Toomey was stirring. Pete grasped him by a shoulder and dragged him upright. They went into the cell block and the men were locked in separate cells. Toomey slumped on to the bunk and closed his eyes. Martin stood at his cell door, gripping the bars, his face showing concern at the adverse turn of the situation.

'Are you lawmen?' Martin demanded. 'We were told none was around.'

'Ritter got it wrong,' Clay said. 'So what have you got to say for yourself?'

Martin shook his head. 'I got nothing to say. If I open my mouth I'll likely put a rope around my neck. There's nothing doing!'

'It's your neck,' Pete observed. 'We'll waste no time on these two, Clay. Put their horses at the back of the jail and then fetch our mounts from the livery barn. We'll ride over to Sunset Ridge and hand these two over to the sheriff. We've got to get Sheriff Cooper in on this as soon as we can.'

'Sure.' Clay nodded. 'I'll go out the back door. 'You stay quiet in here, Pa, in case Edlin shows up for the keys. I'll bring our horses round the back.'

Pete nodded. 'Watch your step, son.'

Clay departed by the back door. He fetched the two horses from the front of the office and tethered them behind the jail before returning to the street and heading for the livery barn. He stepped into an adjacent alley mouth when a rider appeared along the street, and dropped a hand to his gun when he recognized Mike Cade.

He watched Cade with narrowed eyes, wanting to go for him bald-headed, but common sense prevailed for he knew he had to catch Cade in the act of breaking the law to have a chance of proving anything. Cade angled across the street to the right and rode into a wide alley that led to Steve Garrett's freight-line office. Clay crossed the street, flattened himself against the corner of the alley Cade had entered, and peered along its length to see Cade dismounting in front of the office. His eyes glittered as he watched.

So what was Cade up to? The question shimmered in Clay's mind. He watched Cade tether his horse to a hitch rail and then mount the outside steps to the office, which was situated on the first floor of the big warehouse Steve Garrett used to store the merchandise he brought in from Tombstone. Was there a link between Cade and Garrett? Suspicion flared in Clay's mind. He entered the alley and moved forward cautiously, wanting to learn more about Cade's visit.

He saw Cade enter the office. The door was closed, and Clay heaved a sigh. There was no way he could get closer without revealing his presence. He stood for some moments just staring at Garrett's office while he considered the situation. He knew Cade was involved in the trouble, and also Ritter, but knowing was not proof, and he was aware that he needed water-tight evidence against those men if he hoped to convince the sheriff of their guilt.

A gunshot sounded, and Clay started as if he had been struck by a bullet. He whirled around and ran back along the alley to the street, trying to judge the source of the shot by the direction of the fading echoes. He paused in the alley-mouth and looked around. The street was quiet, but a couple of men emerged from the saloon and stood looking in the direction of the law office.

Clay knew real fear as he thought of the situation his father was in, and ran along the street towards the jail. He did not pause when he reached the two men in front of the saloon but called to them in passing.

'Did that shot come from the jail?' he demanded.

'Sounded like it to me,' one of them replied.

Clay ran to the alley beside the jail, aware that the front door of the office was locked on the inside. He drew his pistol as he reached the back door of the jail and thrust it open. Gun cocked, he crossed the threshold into the gloomy interior of the cell block. He saw his father lying on the floor by the door leading into the law office, and a man was standing over him, a gun in his right hand.

The man with the gun straightened and turned to face Clay, who recognized Shorty Allen. The gun Allen was holding began to lift, its black muzzle gaping at Clay. Anger exploded in Clay's mind and he reacted instinctively. He levelled his gun, thumbed back the hammer, and fired without hesitation. The sound of the shot filled the cell block with reverberating thunder and the gun recoiled in his hand.

Allen took the bullet in the centre of his chest and the impact threw him backwards.

Clay felt as if he were caught up in a nightmare. He watched Allen drop his gun and twist to the floor, where he lay on his back, his limbs twitching. A trickle of blood showed on Allen's chest, and the acrid smell of the burned gunpowder brought home to Clay the fact that this was no bad dream but harsh reality.

He was filled with shock as he ran forward and dropped to his knees beside his inert father . . .

5

Pete Overman was unconscious, his eyes closed and his face ashen in shock. Blood was showing on his shirt front. Clay thrust his pistol into its holster and opened his father's shirt. He could hear an urgent hand rattling the front door of the office as he gazed at the neat round hole in Pete's left shoulder. Blood was seeping into the material of Pete's shirt. Clay was horrified by the grim sight. He had no experience of gunshot wounds and feared Pete was dying.

Clay got to his feet and hurried to the back door, intent on fetching Doc Miller. He ran into the alley and collided with a figure coming towards him. They fell apart, and Clay hit the wall and slithered along it to land on his hands and knees in the alley. He pushed himself upright and found Paul Edlin

91

lying on his back in the dust.

'What in hell is going on, Clay?' Edlin demanded, getting to his feet. 'Who fired those shots?'

Clay grasped the undertaker by the front of his shirt and shook him.

'Never mind the questions, Paul. Pete has been shot and is likely to die. Fetch Doc Miller, and hurry it up.'

Edlin opened his mouth to argue, but the expression on Clay's face deterred him and he turned swiftly and ran from the alley. Clay went back into the cell block. He stepped over the inert figure of Shorty Allen and dropped to one knee beside his father. Pete's eyelids flickered. He was groaning softly. Clay was in a ferment of indecision but was aware that there was nothing he could do. He stood up and turned to the cells. Toomey and Martin were standing motionless and silent at their doors, shocked by Shorty Allen's death.

'So what happened here?' Clay demanded. He drew his pistol but was hardly aware of the action as he pointed it menacingly at the men.

'Shorty turned up just after you left,' Martin said. 'He got the drop on your pa but the old man wouldn't give in and grabbed for Shorty's gun, which went off, and your pa fell down. Shorty was looking for the cell keys when you came in.'

'Did you see anything different?' Clay asked Toomey, and the man shook his head silently.

'Let us out of here and we'll split the breeze back to Wichita,' Martin said. 'I didn't like this deal in the first place, and it has turned sour on us.'

'Tell me all about the deal and I might let you go before the sheriff gets here. Who else is mixed up in this? Why was the Bar O picked out for trouble?'

Neither man replied. Clay heard rapid footsteps in the alley outside and turned. Paul Edlin came hurrying in at the back door, followed closely by Doc Miller carrying a medical bag. Miller glanced down at Shorty Allen and stepped over him without a second glance. He dropped to his knees beside Pete and examined him. Clay stood at the doctor's shoulder, watching closely.

Miller's rugged face was beaded with sweat as he pushed himself to his feet. He was short and fleshy; well into middle age. His brown eyes narrowed as he looked at Clay.

'He'll live,' he pronounced. 'But it looks like I'll have to do a big job on him. The bullet is still in there. Paul, call in some men and have Pete carried over to my place.'

Edlin, standing silently in the background, shook himself and turned quickly. He saw townsmen gathering at the back door and called four of them in. Pete was lifted carefully and borne away. Clay began to follow the doctor but Edlin grasped his arm and held him. Clay tried to shake him off but the undertaker held on, his face ugly with determination.

'Not so fast, Clay,' he rasped 'I wanta know what happened in here. Who are those two men in the cells?'

Clay explained tersely and, when he mentioned Snape Ritter, Edlin shook his head in disbelief.

'Are you sure of your facts?' he demanded. 'I know Ritter ain't no great shakes as a deputy, but you're saying he's mixed up in something crooked. Where is he? I wanta hear what he's got to say.'

'He's hiding out of town until these two men get back to him with Pete's body,' Clay insisted. 'You need to get the sheriff over here to check this out. Can you send someone over to Sunset Ridge?'

'Sure I can, but I don't want to bother Bill Cooper unless it is for something serious.'

'So what do you call Pete getting shot? Ain't that serious enough? Get the sheriff over here. This trouble ain't over by a long rope. I'll come back when I know what Pete's condition is. And don't make any mistake about this: those two men in the cells are mighty dangerous.'

95

Edlin shook his head, apparently unconvinced, and Clay departed in a hurry. He reached the street end of the alley and paused, his thoughts racing across the stream of events. Doc Miller had judged that Pete would survive, and the doctor knew a thing or two about bullet wounds. Clay hurried along to the doctor's house, where several men were standing out front waiting for news of Pete Overman's condition.

Clay was surrounded by curious men and beset by a host of questions. He shook his head, pushed his way through them, entered the doctor's house and closed the door resolutely on the babble of voices. The door of Doc's office was open and Clay moved into the doorway to see his father stretched out on the examination couch with Doc Miller bending over him. Pete was stripped to the waist and Mrs Miller was beside him, assisting her husband. She looked up, saw Clay's anxious face, and smiled reassuringly at him.

'Pete will be all right, Clay,' she encouraged.

Doc Miller looked up, a probe in his hand. 'Sure thing, Clay,' he said. 'Why don't you go and get yourself a drink? You sure look like you could use one. Come back in about half an hour and this will be over.'

Clay thought about Mike Cade and nodded. 'OK, Doc,' he replied.

He left the house and went off to Bennett's saloon. Ray Warner, the bartender, took one look at Clay's face and reached for a whiskey bottle.

'So what happened, Clay?' Warner demanded as he poured whiskey into a glass and pushed it towards Clay. 'Have that on the house. Is it true there's a dead man in the jail? Who is he, and who shot him?'

Clay drank the whiskey and asked for a beer to quench his thirst. Warner turned quickly and produced a tall schooner of foaming beer.

'You were in the jail, Clay, so tell me what happened,' Warner persisted. 'I saw you take the law office key off Edlin. What's going on? Your pa was arrested yesterday, and he was in here before Ritter took him, saying the Bar O ranch house had been burned down and the stream dammed.'

'I'll talk to you later, Ray. Right now I got things to do.' Clay drank the beer and set down the glass. He walked to the batwings and departed with Warner's questions ringing in his ears. He was cold inside, and the knowledge that he had shot and killed Shorty Allen did not sit easily in his mind. He made for the alley that led to Garrett's warehouse, pushed by an angry determination to get some answers to the questions plaguing him.

He needed to talk to Mike Cade, and it would be better to get Cade alone somewhere . . .

* * *

When Mike Cade visited Steve Garrett he was determined to push ahead with the next step of his crooked scheme. He watched his surroundings closely as he ascended the steps to the freight-line office, aware that a man couldn't sneeze in Pine Flats without someone noticing and, because of his deviousness, he played the game of not letting his left hand know what his right hand was doing.

He paused at the door of the office, raised his hand to knock, and then shrugged, thrust open the door quickly, and stepped into the dim office. He smiled when Garrett, seated at his desk, looked up with a startled expression on his fleshy face.

'Oh, it's you!' Garrett threw down the pen he was holding and drew a deep breath. 'One of these days you'll bust in on the wrong man and likely collect a bullet for your pains.'

'I don't want anyone but us to know of the business arrangement we have.' Cade closed the door with his right heel. He studied Garrett's over-large figure for a moment, wondering if he had made a mistake in taking the freighter into partnership. 'I've got things moving at last. My three men from Wichita showed up a few days ago and I set them to work on Bar O. They dammed the stream, cut off Overman's water supply, and then burned down the Bar O ranch house.'

He went on to describe Clay Overman's visit to the FT, and Garrett shook his head, his expression showing that he was unimpressed.

'So you finally confronted Clay Overman, huh?' he demanded. 'Is that how you got that bruise on your face? Clay ain't a pushover, and I reckon you're handling him wrong. If you'd used my tactics, the Bar O would be finished now and the ranch house would still be standing, but because you have a personal grudge against Clay you're letting your feelings run away with your common sense. You should have framed Clay and his father with some crime that Ritter could arrest them for. That would have got them safely out of the way and we could have bought Bar O cheaply when it came up for sale.'

'This way, we'll get the place for nothing.' Cade sneered. 'You ain't doing so well in business, Steve, so don't try to tell me how to run mine. I want to see Clay Overman squirm for the beating he gave me when we were kids and I'm gonna torment him to hell and back before I kill him. We're doing OK. Ritter is well and truly on our side and he doesn't know any limits when it comes to lining his pockets. When I saw him a couple of days ago he said he was ready to dry-gulch Clay Overman for a few bucks. But I want that pleasure for myself. I had Clay in my sights last week and fired to miss just to give him a taste of what's coming to him.'

'You'd better be careful you don't over-play it and lose him,' Garrett warned. 'I advise you to cut out the personal stuff and concentrate on the business we planned. This ain't a game we're running. I stand to lose everything if it goes wrong. I need to get out of the freighting business and into cattle ranching. That's why I threw in with you, so let's get to it.'

'The plan is working,' Cade observed. 'There are bigger issues at stake than just putting the Bar O out of business. My uncle Thurlow owns a quarter share of the FT ranch, and I want to take over the other three-quarters from Frank Truscott. I'm working on Sue Truscott, and before I'm through with her she'll be eating out of my hand like a two year old. I owe her something for the way she treated me when I stayed at FT as a youngster — her and her haughty ways and big plans! I've got a score to settle with her for the misery I suffered in those days, and I'll get my own back if it's the last thing I do.'

'It could turn out to be the last thing you do if Clay Overman gets the better of you,' Garrett warned. 'As I see it, you would be better off grabbing FT by marrying the girl. But that's your business. If you want to do everything the hard way then go ahead, but remember I've told you it's the wrong way if it all blows up in your face. Now what do you want? I'm busy right now and can't afford the time just to jaw about this crooked plan when my legitimate business is going downhill fast.'

'I want to know what you think about hitting those nesters north of Bar O and pointing the blame at Clay and Pete Overman.'

'I said it was a good idea when it first came up.' Garrett leaned back from his desk and his chair protested at his shifting weight. 'I've got a couple of good men who would handle that for a few dollars; no questions asked — Jake Moore and Wes Santee — and it would set the wheels in motion quicker than the methods you are using at the moment. Those nesters would hit back at Bar O quicker than forked lightning strikes, and all our troubles would be over if blood was spilled.'

'The more I think about it the better I like it,' Cade mused. 'Are you sure you can trust Moore and Santee?'

'They'll go along with it. They know their jobs are on the line if the freighting business folds, so they're prepared to do anything to help out.'

'How would you handle the deal?'

'Burn a couple of nester cabins, shoot some stock, and leave a plain trail to Bar O.' Garrett shrugged. 'It's as simple as that. Leave it to me and I'll get it up and running. You call off your men for the moment and I'll handle it my way. I can promise you quicker results using my methods.'

'OK. Give it a try.' Cade turned and glanced through the window beside the door. The alley appeared to be deserted but he was taking no chances. 'I'd better leave by your back door. We need to keep our association quiet for as long as possible.'

'Use this inner door and go through the warehouse to the back door,' Garrett said, picking up his pen. 'I suggest in future that you come to my house after dark when you want to talk some more.'

'I'll do that.' Cade walked around the desk and departed.

Garrett sat for a moment, thinking deeply. He shook his head slowly as his thoughts scanned the situation. He was not happy, sensing he would further his own plans more easily without Cade's assistance, and at this moment the thought of dispensing with Cade's murderous plan and substituting his own appealed greatly. His subconscious mind moved rapidly as he resumed his book-keeping . . .

* * *

Clay paused at the steps leading up to Garrett's office, but impatience was pushing in his mind and he ascended quickly. Sweat beaded his forehead and excitement mingled with anticipation in his breast to fill him with a yeasty feeling that sent uncharacteristic emotions through his mind. He had killed a man, and the knowledge lay like a stone in the forefront of his consciousness. More than that, he was aware that he might have to kill again before the trouble sitting on his shoulders was finally dispersed.

He pushed open the door at the top of the steps and entered an office that was austerely furnished. A desk was set in front of an inner door that led down into the warehouse, and Steve Garrett was seated behind the desk; a big, fleshy man of around fifty who looked as if he weighed at least 200 pounds and was carrying most of it around his waist as surplus fat. Garrett looked up quickly at Clay's entrance, and his thick lips pulled tight when he recognized his visitor. His brown eyes narrowed; were almost lost in the network of wrinkles clustered around his eye sockets.

'What can I do for you?' Garrett's husky voice seemed to start in his boots and gather resonance as it rose to his mouth.

Clay, glancing around the otherwise empty office, said: 'Where is Mike Cade.'

'Who in hell is Mike Cade?' Garrett leaned back in his seat and fixed his visitor with a hard stare. 'Have you been drinking, Overman? Whaddya want? I ain't seen a soul all day, I'm busy as all hell, and you come in wasting my time with a fool question.'

'Cade was in here a few minutes ago,' Clay said heavily. He paused before the desk, placed both hands on the paper-strewn surface and leaned his weight on his hands as he leaned forward. 'I saw him come up here so I know you're lying, Garrett. You'd better wise up, but quick. I'm looking for answers to some questions bothering me, and I suspect you can help me, so cut out the innocence act and come clean. Why are you lying about not seeing Cade?'

Garrett pushed himself to his feet and started around the desk, his big hands clenching into ham-like fists.

'Where do you get off, mister — coming in here and accusing me of God knows what? You'd better leave quietly before I throw you out.'

Clay dropped his right hand to the butt of his holstered pistol and drew the weapon with a slick movement as Garrett lifted his left shoulder slightly and prepared to throw a punch. The muzzle of the gun jabbed into Garrett's big paunch, causing him to exhale noisily. Garrett gasped in pain and hunched his shoulders. Clay struck him across the left temple with the muzzle of the pistol and Garrett dropped to his knees like a pole-axed steer, shaking the office with his solid bulk.

'Don't try and get tough with me,' Clay rasped. 'My pa has been shot and I've just killed a man so I'm not playing games. You are lying about Cade, so what have you got to hide, huh?'

A trickle of blood showed on Garrett's temple. His right arm was across a corner of the desk, supporting his upper body, and his legs were bent under him. Clay reached forward with his pistol and pressed the muzzle against Garrett's sweating forehead.

'I am deadly serious,' Clay said tensely, 'so answer my questions. What was Cade doing here and where is he now?'

'I'll have the law on you,' Garrett muttered.

'I'd like nothing better than to see Ritter right now. I heard he's hiding out of town, waiting to learn that my pa has been killed. So what's going on, Garrett? You better spill the beans before I take you apart piece by piece.'

Garrett lifted his head and gazed up at Clay, taking in the steady pistol and Clay's resolute manner.

'I don't know who you are talking about,' he said. 'Sure, I recall there was a caller earlier but I didn't get his name. He was from FT — brought a note from Thurlow Payne, the foreman. Now you better get out of here, Overman. I'll talk to Ritter when I see him. You can't come in here, assault me and get away with it.'

'Show me the note,' Clay persisted. 'I can tell by your face it's not the truth, Garrett, so you better come clean. I ain't leaving here until I get what I need to know. What did Cade want with you?'

Garrett made an attempt to push himself to his feet but failed.

'So you wanta play this the hard way,' Clay observed, lifting his pistol to deliver another blow to Garrett's head. Garrett cringed and raised his right arm to protect his skull. Clay laughed harshly. 'It's gonna get a whole lot worse than this before I'm through with you, Garrett,' he declared. 'There's no law around here so I've got to handle this business myself, and after what has happened to me in the last twenty-four hours I ain't in the mood to fool around.'

'You must be loco, coming in here and throwing your weight around. You won't feel so tough when I buy into your game. You better remember that you started the rough stuff.'

Clay regarded Garrett while he considered the situation. He was aware that Garrett was tough and not ready to crack, and he was not prepared to go further at the moment. He could learn what he needed to know from Cade, who might still be in town, so he holstered his pistol and turned to leave. He paused with the door of the office ajar and looked back at Garrett.

'I ain't finished with you yet,' he warned, 'and the next time I drop on to you I want some real good answers, mister.'

He turned to leave, slamming the office door behind him, and was at the bottom of the steps when he heard the door creak open. He looked up and saw Garrett appearing in the office doorway. The freighter was holding a pistol in his right hand and pointed it down at Clay. The crash of a shot hammered and sent a string of echoes rolling across the town. Clay ducked as the bullet tore a strip of wood out of the handrail at his side. He palmed his gun and cocked it, but Garrett darted back into his office before Clay could return fire.

Clay turned and ascended the steps two at a time. This was more like it, he thought grimly. This was a deadly reaction from Garrett, and exactly what he needed. He lunged at the office door and shouldered it open, his gun lifting as he blundered in through the doorway. He paused when he found the office deserted. The inner door stood ajar, and Clay halted his headlong rush and moved forward cautiously. It looked as if he had made a break-through in this trouble, and he was eager to take full advantage of the situation.

He eased around the inner door and peered down the flight of steps leading into the warehouse. A gun blasted from below and a bullet plunked into the woodwork beside his head. Clay clenched his teeth. He had bought chips in this deadly game and now had to play the hand that had been dealt.

6

Clay pushed his gun hand forward, ready to trade lead. He could see gunsmoke rising from a stack of crates down on the warehouse floor and kept low as he eased forward. The gun below fired again, from a different position, and Clay ducked as a slug whined past his head. He returned fire at the puff of smoke which marked Garrett's position. The thunder of the shots filled his ears and the stink of cordite assailed his nostrils. He started down the steps, gun uplifted and ready for action, his heart pounding erratically in excitement.

Garrett's head and shoulders appeared above a stack of wooden boxes and he thrust his pistol into view, squeezing the trigger to send a string of shots at Clay. The ominous crackle of closely passing lead around him filled Clay with desperation and he jumped off the steps to land heavily on the warehouse floor. He rolled behind a stack of crates and pushed himself upright, eager to continue the fight.

The instant Clay revealed his position two more guns cut loose at him from different parts of the big warehouse and he ducked swiftly. He heard Garrett shouting orders and realized that some of the freighter's men had joined in the fight. He stayed low and looked around. The odds against him were too great and he knew that he had to get out while he still could.

He saw a window to his left and eased towards it. A gun was firing unsighted in his direction to keep his head down, and he guessed Garrett was pressing forward to get a clear shot at him. He lifted his Colt to return fire and the hammer clicked on an empty chamber. He holstered his gun, picked up a wooden box, and hurled it through the window. He followed it quickly in a low dive that took him out through the aperture. Slugs whined around him but he was in the clear. He fell heavily on his left shoulder, sprang up and darted into cover.

Clay ducked behind a stack of empty crates but did not pause. He was wearing a leather gunbelt, not a cartridge belt, and had no spare shells for his pistol. Shots came at him from the broken window. He threw himself around a corner of the warehouse, gained his feet, and ran into the alley that led to the main street. His ears protested at the crash of shots but he had not been touched by the questing lead.

Men were coming out on the street in response to the sound of shooting. Clay ran to the gun shop, intent on getting more shells. He dived around a group of men, who shouted questions at him, but he ignored them and kept running. A moment later a gun fired from the alley he had just left and a bullet thudded into a shop front close by. Boots pounded the sidewalk as the watching townsmen hunted cover. Clay reached the door of the gun shop and bustled through it.

The shop was deserted, and the door leading to the back room of the shop was ajar. Clay called for Amos Berry but there was no reply. He ran around the glass-topped counter and snatched up a box of .45 cartridges, ripped it open and drew his gun to reload it, thumbing brass shells into the chambers of the cylinder. Boots pounded the sidewalk outside and he closed the pistol with it only half-loaded. The door of the shop was thrust open and Wes Santee came lumbering in, a drawn pistol in his hand.

Clay dropped to one knee as Santee levelled the gun. He worked his own weapon and triggered a shot as Santee fired. Santee jumped convulsively, as if he had been branded with a hot iron. Clay heard a slug screech past his left ear. Santee pulled up in midstride, dropped his gun and clutched at his chest, then twisted sharply to fall inertly on his face in the doorway.

The solid reverberations of the shooting in such close confines sounded like thunder. Clay remained motionless, gun upraised and cocked, listening intently for other footsteps on the sidewalk. His ears were ringing from the crash of the shots and he swallowed to clear his hearing. A sigh gusted from him and he pushed to his feet and went over to where Santee was crumpled. Blood was trickling from the man's chest, and Clay could tell at a glance that he was dead. He bent and picked up Santee's discarded gun and stuck it in his own holster.

Shock swamped Clay's mind. He had known Santee well; they had often passed the time of day, and now Santee was dead. What was going on? It seemed the trouble that had descended upon Bar O was more far-reaching than it had at first appeared. Clay forced his mind to concentrate on the situation. Santee was one of Steve Garrett's men, and there were others apparently ready to kill on Garrett's orders.

He heard a sound at his back and whirled to see Amos Berry emerging from the back of his shop. Berry's jaws were champing as if he had been caught eating a meal, and his face was pale and drawn in shock. He gazed in disbelief at the body of Santee. His jaw stopped chewing and he swallowed noisily.

'Say, what in hell is going on, Clay?' Berry demanded. 'I was snatching a bite to eat when all hell broke loose.'

'I don't have the time to tell you, Amos,' Clay responded as he stepped into the doorway of the shop to look out around the street. Men were gathering here and there in little knots, all talking excitedly and looking around as if anticipating more shooting. Clay saw Steve Garrett and Jake Moore coming along the sidewalk, guns in their hands, and Garrett was talking animatedly to every man he passed, evidently giving his own version of what was happening.

Clay turned back into the shop, picked up the box of shells and hurriedly filled his pockets with its contents. There was a side door that gave access to the alley beside the law office, and he skirted around the motionless gunsmith and departed quickly, aware that he would have to face Garrett again, but he was disinclined to continue the fight immediately. He needed time in which to consider the situation, and wanted badly to get his hands on Mike Cade.

He turned to the back lots and hurried along the alley to its end. A gun crashed at his back as he turned out of the alley and a bullet smacked into a wall. He twisted, peered back around the corner, and saw Garrett and Moore standing at the street end of the alley. Both men fired and gunsmoke drifted along the alley. Clay lifted his gun and sent two quick shots in reply.

Then he waited, and when the smoke had cleared he saw no sign of his adversaries. He went along the back of the jail, pausing when he noticed that Toomey and Martin's horses were not where he had left them. He turned into the next alley and paused at the rear door of the cell block, which was standing ajar. He pushed it open. Shorty Allen's body was still on the floor inside, but the cells that had held Toomey and Martin were empty.

Clay sighed as he gazed at the cells. Damn Paul Edlin! The undertaker had not believed his version of what had happened, and now Toomey and Martin were free. The thought came to Clay then that perhaps the two men would attempt to finish the job they had come into town to do, and fear for his father spurted into his mind. He ran back to the alley and hurried towards the doctor's house.

He watched for signs of Garrett and Moore as he crossed the street but evidently the big freighter had changed his tactics and was nowhere in sight. Groups of men were standing around, particularly in front of the saloon, and Clay heard his name called several times but did not turn aside. He needed to check that his father was all right.

Paul Edlin was coming out of the doctor's house as Clay reached it.

'Doc says Pete is gonna be OK,' Edlin said. 'Give him a couple of weeks and he'll be up and about again.'

'You turned Toomey and Martin loose after I told you they came into town to kill Pete,' Clay accused.

'Now hold your horses, Clay. You can't go around arresting anyone, no matter what you think they might have done. I had to turn them loose because I've got no evidence against them. They promised to ride straight out of town, and I stood and watched them go.'

'Yeah, and I'll bet they went no further than the end of the street!' Bitterness sounded in Clay's voice. 'But now you've got another problem. I just killed Wes Santee in the gun shop. It was self-defence. Steve Garrett turned his men loose on me after I went to his office. We traded lead in his warehouse before the fight spilled over on to the street. You'll find Santee's body in the doorway of the gun shop. So what are you gonna do about that — arrest me?'

'Did anyone see the shooting?' Edlin demanded.

'I didn't have time to arrange for witnesses to be present,' Clay countered.

Edlin shook his head and went on his way, leaving Clay to gaze after him in disbelief. It came to Clay that perhaps Edlin was against Bar O in this trouble, and he entered the doctor's house to find his father resting on the couch in Miller's office, evidently asleep. Mrs Miller was present, and she smiled reassuringly at Clay.

'It's good news, Clay. Your father will be all right. The bullet has been removed and, barring complications, he should make a complete recovery.'

'Thanks, Mrs Miller,' Clay responded. 'I'm obliged to you for helping Pa. Can he be moved? If he can then I'll take him along to the hotel when he wakes up.'

'He'll be unconscious for a while yet,'

Mrs Miller replied. 'You'd better leave him where he is at least until tomorrow morning. I'm certain Doc will want to keep an eye on him until then.'

'I'm worried that a couple of killers will make another try for him. They've been turned loose from the jail.'

'Have you spoken to Snape Ritter about that?'

'Ritter has left town and won't be coming back for a while. I can't leave Pa here unguarded if there is any risk to him, and I also need to track down a man who I think is behind our trouble.'

'Doc isn't here right now. He was called out to another shooting along the street.'

'He won't be needed there,' Clay observed harshly. 'That's a job for the undertaker.'

Doc Miller returned at that moment, and paused in the doorway of his office to gaze searchingly at Clay.

'Edlin is fixing to arrest and jail you, Clay. He's trying to gather a posse to come for you. What's going on? Did you shoot Santee?'

'Yeah, in self-defence,' Clay responded. 'Steve Garrett turned his men loose on me because I discovered he is mixed up in the trouble Bar O is getting.'

'Garrett has reported that you attacked him and started the shooting.'

'He would say that.' Clay shook his head. 'And I wouldn't be surprised if you believed him because I find it difficult to accept the half of what has happened since yesterday.'

'I'm only interested in the well-being of my patients,' Miller said. 'The dead man in the jail shot Pete, didn't he?'

'That's right. I walked in there after hearing a shot and found the dead man, Shorty Allen, standing over Pa with a gun in his hand. He turned the gun on me but I beat him to it.'

'There were two men locked in the jail; where do they come into it?'

Clay explained the events leading up to the shooting and Miller shook his head.

'I don't understand the half of it,

Clay, but I've known Pete for years and always found him to be honest and hard-working. I'll go along with your version for now. Do you think there is a danger that someone will show up here to finish Pete?'

'That's right. Either Steve Garrett and his men, or those two who were in jail.'

'No one will harm a patient of mine while he is in my care,' Miller said firmly. 'You better leave, Clay, and look out for yourself. I won't let anything bad happen to Pete. Get moving, son! I don't want any shooting on my doorstep, and they'll be coming here for you. Edlin is not a man I admire. He's got a mind like a mule, and if he reckons you're in the wrong he won't budge an inch either way in his thinking.'

'Thanks, Doc.' Clay turned to leave, but Miller grasped his arm.

'Use the back door, Clay. I can hear Edlin's voice out front. Leave him to me.'

Clay turned and hurried through the house to the rear door. He drew his gun and checked the back lot before leaving, and there was a strange tingling sensation between his shoulder blades as he ran from the area. He wanted to confront Mike Cade, but could not ignore the danger of Toomey and Martin being free in the town. He kept to the back lots until he reached Garrett's warehouse, entered the building by its rear door, and made his way to the stairs leading up to Garrett's office.

He pushed open the inner door of the office and peered inside just as the outer door was thrust open. He lifted his gun when Jake Moore, Garrett's righthand man, entered the office. Moore was not expecting trouble, and crossed the threshold before spotting Clay's ominous figure. He pulled up short, his expression changing, and then made as if to draw his pistol. Clay was holding his gun in his hand, and the sound of it being cocked froze

Moore into immobility.

'Kind of surprised you, huh?' Clay demanded. 'Get your hands up and move away from the door.' He waited until Moore had complied. 'So where is Garrett? He should be here to face the music, seeing he's behind this trouble.'

'I don't know where he's gone.' Moore shrugged. 'He left me on the street.'

Clay moved in beside Moore and lifted a pistol out of the man's holster. 'You're the lucky one,' he observed. 'Santee came at me shooting and I killed him. So now you can tell me what's going on. What triggered Garrett into action, and where does he fit into this trouble I'm getting from Mike Cade?'

'I don't know a thing about that. All I do know is that Garrett came down into the warehouse from his office and told me and Santee to be ready for trouble. The next minute you came out of the office and started shooting. We only joined in because you fired at us.'

Clay heard the sound of a boot on the outside stairs and half turned to face the door. Moore moved at the same time. His right hand shot out and grasped Clay's gun wrist. He shouted for help as he forced the muzzle of the weapon away from his body. Clay kept turning, dragging Moore around with him, and he was facing the door with Moore in front of him when it was shouldered open and Rafe Toomey came blundering into the office.

Toomey had a drawn pistol in his hand and levelled it only to find himself covering Moore. Clay threw his left arm around Moore's neck, held him close, and tore his gun wrist out of Moore's grasp. He thrust the weapon towards Toomey, who tried desperately to throw himself sideways out of the line of fire. Moore struck at Clay's gun with his free hand but it exploded before he could divert it. The office shook as the shot rang out.

Toomey paused like a dancer teetering on the edge of a precipice. The

128

bullet struck him in the chest, its impact throwing him to one side. He fell heavily with blood spurting. Clay swung the pistol upwards and slammed it solidly against Moore's skull. Moore groaned and slid to the floor. Clay saw Sim Martin appear in the outer doorway of the office and shifted his aim quickly, but Martin hurled himself out through the doorway and vanished, his boots clattering on the outside steps.

Clay eased sideways to the window beside the door and looked out. He saw Martin jump down the last few steps to land heavily in the dust before springing up and running desperately for the cover of the alley. As Clay turned away from the window he spotted Paul Edlin leading two townsmen out of the alley to head towards the office. Edlin was carrying a double-barrelled shotgun, and looked as if he had every intention of using it.

Clay retreated to the inner stairs and descended into the warehouse. His ears were ringing from the crash of gunfire and he swallowed several times to relieve the pressure that had built up inside his head. He left the warehouse at a run and sought an alley which would give him access to the street closer to the livery barn, aware that he could do nothing more around Pine Flats. Steve Garrett would have to wait. He had an urgent reckoning with Mike Cade, and it was time he confronted the man he knew to be causing the trouble that had erupted around Bar O.

The street was deserted when Clay peered out of the alley and gazed around. An air of menace seemed to hang in the still air. The familiar surroundings of the town had taken on an edge of hostility and he knew every man around would be against him, thanks to Paul Edlin. He left the alley and headed for the livery barn at a run, gun in hand and ready for use. He reached the front of the barn and paused to look around. His eyes narrowed when he saw Edlin and two of the townsmen emerging from the alley that led to Garrett's freight office.

Edlin raised his shotgun and fired both barrels although he was out of range. Clay saw dust fly up in the street several yards in front of him and heard buckshot flying through the air around him. He dashed for the wide doorway of the barn as two pistols began shooting, and chunks of lead smacked solidly into the sun-warped door beside him.

Walt Massey, the liveryman, was emerging from his dusty office, attracted by the shooting.

'What's the trouble, Clay?' he demanded.

'I wish I knew the half of it,' Clay countered. 'Saddle my sorrel for me, Walt. I've got to get out of here, but fast. Have you seen Mike Cade around in the last half-hour?'

'He's Thurlow Payne's nephew, huh? Yeah I saw him about ten minutes ago. I was up in the loft doorway taking in hay when he galloped out of town like his tail was on fire. He sure was raising dust. I'd heard some shooting shortly before that and wondered what was going on so I watched him leaving. He got just clear of town when he met a rider coming in, and damned if he didn't start a ruckus right there on the trail. He hit the rider with his fist, knocked her out of the saddle, then bundled her across her horse and headed for other parts with her.'

'Her?' Clay questioned. 'It was a woman he met?'

'I couldn't swear to that,' Massey said. 'It sure looked like a woman, small and shapely, and I recognized the horse. It was the paint Sue Truscott rides.'

'And you did nothing about it?' Clay demanded.

'What could I do?' Massey countered. 'I know Ritter ain't around, so who else could I tell? And I'm too old to get mixed up in any trouble. So what is going on?'

'Just saddle my horse for me and I'll go check on Sue,' Clay rasped. 'Make it quick, Walt. I've had more than my share of trouble around here today.'

He turned back to survey the street as the liveryman hurried to saddle his horse and saw Edlin advancing grimly towards the barn with his two townsmen spread out beside him. Clay levelled his pistol and fired three shots, aiming high, and the trio scattered for cover, firing recklessly as they fled. Clay grimaced as he waited, his mind barely registering the strike of the slugs in the barn door. His thoughts were on Sue, and he was racked by anger, which boded ill for Mike Cade.

Edlin must have decided to call off his manhunt, for Clay saw the undertaker running back along the nearer sidewalk to get away from the livery barn. Moments later the two men who had been backing Edlin also pulled out. Some of the pressure seeped away from Clay and he heaved a sigh. He was sweating, tired and hungry, and his throat was clogged by thirst and gunsmoke. But there could be no peace for him. Sue was in trouble and he had to get to her.

He continued to watch the street until Walt Massey called to tell him the sorrel was ready for travel. He checked the street one last time and saw Garrett and Sim Martin emerging together from an alley. Edlin moved into view from the batwings of Bennett's saloon, called to Garrett, and the two men met in the centre of the street. Edlin waved his hands as he spoke and, when he pointed towards the livery barn, Garrett drew his gun, spoke sharply to Martin, and both men began approaching the stable, their guns ready for action.

Clay wasted no more time. He turned away from the doorway, took the reins of his sorrel from the liveryman's hands, and led the animal to the back door.

'Thanks, Walt,' he said. 'I'll settle up with you another time. Right now I've got to split the breeze. Steve Garrett is coming along here with a gunnie and you'll be doing me a big favour if you don't mention Cade and Sue or tell them where I'm going.'

'My lips are sealed, Clay. Go on and hit the trail to find that gal. She could be in a whole lot of trouble right now.'

Clay departed. He led the sorrel out the back door, swung into the saddle and headed out at a run. He did not like leaving his father unprotected, but Sue obviously needed his help. He urged his horse into its fastest pace, and galloped along the lonely trail in pursuit of Mike Cade.

7

Steve Garrett was beset by fear as he and Sim Martin walked to the stable. It seemed to Garrett that the whole shooting works had blown up in his face after Mike Cade had left his office earlier. Clay Overman had shocked him by turning up and accusing him of taking a hand in Cade's crooked plans, and he was aware that he needed to silence Clay before the truth got out. He spoke harshly to Sim Martin, disenchanted with Cade's choice of associates, but his own men had proved almost useless against Clay Overman's response to trouble.

'Sneak around to the back door, Martin,' he ordered. 'Overman is probably in here waiting for us to show up. See if you can get a clear shot at him from behind.'

'OK. Just be careful if we get him

between us not to throw lead at me,' Martin warned, and headed for an alley beside the barn.

Garrett reached the doorway of the barn and flattened himself beside the aperture. His hands were sweating and fear was vibrant in his mind. His whole world had seemed to crash around him when Clay had started shooting. He cursed Cade for not taking precautions against setbacks. The Bar O take-over should have been handled out of town and secretly, as he had advised repeatedly. But Cade apparently had a vendetta going against Clay Overman and wanted to extract the maximum of pleasure from killing Clay. His failure to handle the job properly had resulted in bloodshed in the town, with half the townsfolk being aware of what was going on.

He thrust his gun forward and slid around the door of the barn to enter the dim interior. There was no movement anywhere and he placed his back against a post and waited for Martin to show up at the rear. If Clay was still in the barn they would have him between them. He heard a sound to his right and whirled in that direction, his pistol lifting.

Walt Massey emerged from his office cradling a shotgun in his arms. He paused and covered Garrett.

'What are you up to, Garrett?' Massey demanded. His usually serene face carried a harsh expression as he levelled his weapon at Garrett's fleshy figure.

'I saw Clay Overman come in here,' Garrett replied. 'Where is he? Point that gun somewhere else, Walt.'

'I ain't seen hide nor hair of him. I don't keep a tally of the men who come and go through here. Why are you hunting him?'

'He's killed two men that I'm aware of, one being Wes Santee, but there's been shooting all over town so there could be others down in the dust. No one is safe while Clay is running loose; so where is he?'

'I ain't seen him since he left his horse a couple of hours ago.'

'Well, take a look around and see if his sorrel is still here. I saw him come in and he didn't come out again.'

'I got a better idea. If you want him then you look for him. I don't want to get caught up in any shooting spree. What started the ruckus in the first place?'

'I ain't got time to go into that right now. And I told you to point that gun away from me, Walt.'

Massey shook his head. 'You better get out of here. I don't want any trouble in my barn.'

Garrett caught a movement out of the corner of his eye and turned his head to see Martin coming in at the back door, gun in hand. Martin paused to look around. His gaze fell upon Massey, and when he saw the levelled shotgun he squeezed his trigger. His pistol blasted and Massey dropped his shotgun and fell forward on to his face. Garrett flinched at the sound of the echoing shot.

'Why in hell did you shoot him?' he demanded, as Martin approached.

'It looked like he was getting set to blast you with that shotgun,' Martin protested. 'Is he dead?'

'It sure looks like it.'

'So you tell everyone that Overman killed him before riding out.' Martin grinned. 'That should be good enough to hang him.'

'Say, that's a real good idea.' Garrett nodded. 'Why didn't I think of that? Take a look out front and see if your shot is bringing anyone here.'

Martin went to the door and peered out. 'There's no one around,' he said. 'That Edlin feller has given up, it looks like. What do we do now?'

'I've got to stick around town, but you better ride out and see if you can run down Overman. Kill him if you do, and then hunt up Cade and tell him what's happened. I've got to round up some help and take care of Pete Overman.'

'Sure!' Martin holstered his gun and left the barn.

Garrett suppressed a sigh and looked around before making for the street. He holstered his gun and walked towards the saloon, where half-a-dozen townsmen were standing. He saw Paul Edlin talking to the men, and the undertaker seemed to be trying unsuccessfully to whip up some enthusiasm for a manhunt.

'So what happened at the barn?' Edlin demanded when Garrett reached him.

'You should ask,' Garrett replied. 'Why didn't you close in on Clay Overman when you were after him? When he fired a shot, you and your men turned tail. So that's how the law is run around here now, huh?'

'We were no match for him and I didn't want to get anyone else killed,' Edlin said, shaking his head. 'I'd like to know what set Clay off on a killing spree. Something sure upset him. Did you get him in the barn?'

'No. He was fixing to ride out when I walked in on him and he fired a shot which hit Walt Massey.'

'Jeez!' Edlin gasped. 'Is Massey dead?'

'I didn't check him! Overman rode out on that sorrel of his before I could get a clear shot at him. I've sent a man out to try and track him down, but you'll need to get a posse on his trail.'

'I wish Ritter was around,' Edlin said. 'I'm not a regular lawman and I don't know how to handle this. I've never had any trouble before when I've stood in for Ritter. Where in hell has he gone? He's the one should be here handling this.'

'While you're complaining about the hole you're in Clay Overman is getting clean away. That won't sit well with Bill Cooper when he gets to hear about it. I've got to get some more men together. I heard there are a couple more dead men in my office. I sent Jake Moore back there after Santee was killed chasing Overman, and two men from out of town were going into my office to find work when Overman killed one of them. The other one escaped and I met him on the street. He told me what happened in my office and I've given him a job. He went into the livery barn with me, and that's when Overman shot Massey.'

'Who is the guy you hired?' Edlin demanded. 'Where is he now?'

'He's Sim Martin, and I sent him out to trail Overman. With any luck, when he gets back, we'll know where Overman is. You'd better clean up the town, Edlin, and have a posse ready to ride when Martin returns.'

'What are you going to do?' Edlin demanded. Garrett shook his head. 'I was trying to catch up on my paperwork when Overman dropped in on me so I'll be in my office if you want me. Take a hold of yourself, Edlin, and get things moving.'

Edlin cursed mildly under his breath and turned away. Garrett crossed the street and went to his office. He kept his hand close to his holstered gun as he ascended the steps, and froze for a heart-stopping moment when he saw Rafe Toomey's inert figure lying across the threshold. He ascertained that Toomey was dead before stepping over the body, and then he halted in mid-stride for Jake Moore was slumped on the chair behind the desk.

Moore was holding his head in his hands. He seemed to be only semi-conscious. Garrett went to Moore's side, grasped him by the shoulder, and shook him callously.

'What the hell are you doing skulking in here while Overman is hightailing it out of town?' Garrett demanded. 'Is this what I pay you for? What happened here?'

Moore lifted his head from his hands. He had a big discoloured bruise on his right temple. The skin was broken and blood was seeping from the wound. His eyes were filled with shock and pain, and seemed unable to focus properly.

'What do you think happened, for God's sake?' Moore retorted. 'I walked in on Overman and he got the better of me. Those two men Cade sent to help you came in and Overman shot one of them. Then he cracked me across the skull with his pistol. I don't know how long I've been out, but he sure gave me a whack.'

'Get yourself a horse and ride out of town to the north. Overman took out in that direction, and I want him dead, so rattle your hocks and get moving. Don't come back until you've finished him.'

'You've got to be kidding! Hell, I can't see straight at the moment. I need to visit the doctor. Mebbe he can give me something that'll put me right.'

'Well, make it quick. We have to consider killing Pete Overman or we'll be in bad trouble. He knows what's going on now, and we've got to finish him.'

Moore cursed and struggled to his feet, holding a hand to his head. He leaned against the door post when he reached it, his knees buckling. His head was lowered as if it had become too heavy to hold erect.

'Take a hold,' Garrett snapped. 'Come on. I'll go with you to the doc's place. Pete Overman is there and we've got to finish him off. Get moving, and don't fall down the steps.'

'You're gonna kill Pete Overman in the doc's house?' Moore demanded, in a shocked tone.

'We'll be finished around here if we don't close a few mouths permanent. Cade made a mess of things by going for Clay Overman for personal reasons and now we've got to pick up the pieces. It's a good thing Ritter is in this with us, but the damn fool ain't anywhere to be found right now.'

'Mebbe he's got more sense than us and has headed for other parts. We can't just walk into the doc's place and kill Pete Overman. Doc wouldn't let you pull a trick like that. What will you do if Doc tries to stop you — kill him as well? Doc's wife is always at home, so what will you do if she sees you? She'll talk, sure as hell. Are you fixing to kill her too?'

'Listen, Jake. It's all gone haywire, like a runaway wagon, and we've got to get back on track, but fast. I'll wipe out half this town if that's what it takes to put matters right. Our only alternative is to make a run for it, and then I'll lose everything, and I mean everything.'

'I don't want any part of it,' Moore said through his teeth.

'Huh, you don't have a choice. You're in this up to your neck whether you like it or not, so come on. If we act fast we can stop the rot, but turn yellow now and we're done for.'

'I don't like the thought of killing Doc and his wife,' Moore protested.

'OK, I'll handle them if it has to be done. You take care of Pete Overman and we'll be in the clear.'

Moore lurched forward and left the office. He started for the alley leading to the street but Garrett grasped his arm.

'Not that way so everyone can see us,' he rasped. 'We'll go along the back lots.'

They made their way to the rear of the doctor's house. Moore halted when he reached the back door, and shied away like a fractious horse.

'I can't go through with this,' he muttered.

'We got no choice,' Garrett urged. He tried the door and it opened to his touch. 'Just do like I say. Go straight up the stairs, find Pete Overman and kill him. Use that knife you always carry. I'll wait at the bottom of the stairs and stop anyone coming up. Do this right and we can walk out afterwards and no one will know who did the killing. Now get moving.'

Garrett pushed Moore forward and they entered the kitchen. Garrett inched open an inner door and led the way into the passage that led right through to the front door. The house was silent and still. Garrett drew his gun and cocked it. He motioned Moore forward and they paused at the bottom of the stairs. Moore hesitated again and Garrett waved his pistol threateningly.

'Go on, get on with it,' he rasped in an undertone.

Moore shook his head but ascended the stairs. Garrett stepped back into the space under the stairs to conceal his fleshy figure. He could hear Moore's slow, furtive progress into the upper region of the house. Doc Miller's voice sounded suddenly, coming from one of the two front downstairs rooms, and Mrs Miller answered him. Garrett shrank back; tightened his grip on his pistol, his hand sweating, and hoped he would not have to kill the doctor and his wife. But he was aware that he could not leave any witnesses alive.

Pete Overman was lying in a back bedroom, barely awake and suffering pain from the bullet wound in his left shoulder, which was swathed in heavy bandaging. He was naked from the waist upwards, his right hand under the bedcovers and his left arm resting across his chest in a sling. He heard the door opening, and was surprised when Jake Moore looked into the room. They knew each other well, but had never been close friends. Moore entered the room and closed the door.

'How are you feeling, Pete?' Moore asked, as he crossed to the side of the bed, a taut smile on his face.

'Not too good,' Pete replied. 'My shoulder hurts like hell. What was all that shooting around town? Is Clay in any trouble?'

'I ain't seen Clay, but I heard he was mixed up in the shooting. I don't know what's going on, Pete. Do you know what the trouble is all about? Someone said your ranch house was burned down yesterday. Is that a fact?'

'Yeah, and our stream was dammed just this side of Water Gully. I reckon it was the work of those dang nesters north-east of our range. If you see Clay around, tell him to come and see me. I need to talk to him real urgent.'

'Sure, I'll do that.' Moore reached around to the back of his belt and grasped the bone handle of the long-bladed knife he always carried in a leather sheath. He gritted his teeth, drew the weapon, and swung his hand up above his shoulder for one quick stab at the motionless man in the bed.

Pete saw the quick lift of the hand, spotted the knife, and lifted his right hand from under the bed covers. He was holding a cocked .41 two-shot derringer and squeezed the trigger instantly. The small gun blasted, filling the room with thunder, and the slug smacked solidly into the centre of Moore's chest as the knife began to descend. The impact threw Moore back a step and he shouted in agony as he twisted and fell to the floor, his knife dropping harmlessly from his nerveless hand.

Pete drew a deep smoke-laden breath into his lungs. He had doubted Doc Miller's wisdom in giving him the gun when he regained his senses after having the bullet removed from his left shoulder, but Miller had insisted that his life was in danger and he had to be ready to defend himself.

Steve Garrett, startled by the shot, crouched lower under the stairs, cursing Moore for chickening out from using his knife and resorting to a gun. He was ready to flee, but waited impatiently for Moore to rejoin him. The next instant the door of the right-hand downstairs room was jerked open and Doc Miller appeared. He was holding a pistol and ascended the stairs two at a time. Garrett grimaced; turned swiftly to leave the house by the back door. He holstered his gun and ran fast back to his office.

Doc Miller opened the bedroom door, his gun cocked. He halted on the threshold of the room when he saw Jake Moore stretched out on the floor beside the bed, and then looked into the muzzle of the small gun in Pete Overman's hand . . .

'What the hell happened, Pete?' Miller demanded, putting his pistol into his pocket and dropping to one knee beside the inert Moore.

'He suddenly pulled a knife,' Pete

replied, 'but I was ready for him, thanks to you, Doc. I was suspicious of him because he had no reason to visit me. So what in hell is going on? I sure wish Clay was here to fill me in on what's happening.'

'I've got a nasty feeling that Clay's got his hands full at the moment,' Miller replied as he arose. 'Moore is dead. So why was he in here trying to kill you, Pete?'

'He works for Steve Garrett,' Pete mused.

'And Clay killed another of Garrett's men in the gun shop earlier — Wes Santee. I got a report from witnesses that Santee shot at Clay on the street. Clay ducked into the shop and Santee went after him. And Santee worked for Steve Garrett, so you're not the only one wondering what's going on, Pete. I sure wish that no-good deputy was in town but Ritter disappeared just before all this trouble started. I told Edlin earlier to send a man over to Sunset Ridge to warn the sheriff that we're having trouble. You'd better keep that gun handy, Pete, and I'll fetch Edlin to haul Moore out of here.'

'Let me have your six-shooter, Doc. There ain't but one shot left in the derringer, and the next time there might be two men trying to put my lights out.'

Miller smiled grimly and handed over his gun, taking the derringer in exchange.

'I'll tell Millie to sing out before she enters this room again, Pete,' Miller said in leaving. 'Try to rest now.'

Miller found his wife standing anxiously at the bottom of the stairs. Her face was pale. She compressed her lips when Miller explained what had occurred, and he took hold of her hand and led her back into the big sitting-room.

'I've got to go out, Millie,' he told her. 'Make sure all the doors are locked, and don't open to anyone but me. I'll sing out when I return.'

His wife nodded, and Miller departed.

He stood on the street looking around, wondering what could possibly happen next. The town seemed quiet — too quiet, he thought. A couple of men were standing in front of the law office, looking in his direction, and two saddle horses were standing hip-shot at a rail in front of Bennett's saloon. He shook his head and went along to the law office.

The two men standing on the sidewalk in front of the office were Frank Griffin and Toll Blake, a couple of the townsmen who acted as possemen as and when required by the law. They both peered suspiciously at Miller, as if they thought he had fired the shot they'd heard.

'Did you hear a shot, Doc?' Blake asked.

'Sure did,' Miller replied, and pushed past them to enter the office.

Paul Edlin was alone in the office, seated at the cluttered desk situated at the back of the office by an alley window. The undertaker-cum-lawman looked harassed as he leaned back in his seat, shaking his head and gazing silently at the doctor.

'This has got all too much for me, Doc,' he admitted. 'I'm resigning from this job when Ritter gets back. I'm not cut out for hunting down hardcases — my job is to bury them when they get themselves killed.'

'It does take a special kind of man to handle the law in these benighted times,' Miller agreed. 'Have you sent word to Sheriff Cooper as I advised earlier?'

'Sure. Dave Swanston rode out for Sunset Ridge about an hour ago. But the sheriff won't get here until tomorrow morning at the earliest — if he comes at all.'

'He'd better come.' Miller said. 'Did you hear a shot a few minutes ago?'

'No.' Edlin's haggard face turned grim, and his mouth gaped when the doctor told him what had occurred. 'This is like a nightmare,' he declared. 'What the hell is going on? Why should Jake Moore try to kill Pete Overman?

Say, Moore worked for Steve Garrett like Santee did, and Santee was trying to kill Clay Overman earlier.'

'And you went out hunting Clay without trying to find out what was behind the shooting,' Miller rebuked mildly. 'You've got to change your tactics, Paul. The best thing you can do now is find out if Steve Garrett's got anything to say about all this trouble.'

'I'm not doing anything more until the sheriff gets here,' Edlin said obstinately. 'I've had enough of this trouble.'

'I'll leave that decision to your conscience, Paul, but do something about Jake Moore lying dead in one of my bedrooms. Mrs Miller is particular about that sort of thing. She doesn't mind about the wounded people we put up occasionally, and she helps to nurse them, but she draws the line at dead men cluttering up the place.'

'I'll send my men around immediately.' Edlin got quickly to his feet, his face showing relief at having something positive to do. 'Leave it to me, Doc.'

'I'll go with you to see Steve Garrett if you'd like some company,' Miller persisted. 'I would sure like to know why both his men were killed today trying to murder Pete and Clay Overman.'

8

Clay left Pine Flats at a gallop. He was greatly concerned about Sue, for Walt Massey's account of Mike Cade accosting the girl and taking her away from town filled him with disquiet. He slowed to study the trail when he was clear of town, and soon came to a spot where fresh tracks showed two horses had met and paused together. Clay was adept at reading the muddled tracks in the dust and recognized one set of prints as belonging to the paint Sue always rode. He knew the hoofprints as well as he knew the palm of his hand, and went on at a run when he picked up the direction two horses had taken back away from the town.

What was Cade up to? Why had he forced Sue to ride with him? Walt Massey said Cade had struck the girl before leading her away and, knowing

Cade, Clay could only fear for Sue's safety for he was aware that she would not willingly accompany Cade anywhere. The fact that the two sets of tracks left the trail almost immediately to cut across undulating range served only to heighten Clay's concern for the girl.

Clay switched his attention from the tracks to glance ahead for a sight of riders in the distance, but nothing moved up ahead and he pushed on, traversing a seemingly deserted, silent land, aware that Cade was forcing a fast pace into the wilderness. Clay feared the man had nothing but hostile intentions in his scheming mind.

Thinking of Sue as he followed the tracks, Clay was surprised to discover that his hard attitude towards the girl had been completely reversed since seeing her at the FT earlier. He was aware now how Big Frank had overwhelmed him over the years with his regularly applied mental games of superiority and belittlement which had caused Clay's natural feelings for the girl to recede, but Cade's return to the FT and the subsequent trouble had loosened the mental shackles in Clay's mind and he felt like a swimmer breaking surface into relieving sunlight after a particularly deep and prolonged dive into dark, unfathomable depths. He longed to see Sue and explain his uncertainty.

The two sets of prints seemed to go on forever, leading deeper into the desolation of the range, avoiding well-marked trails and the smaller cattle ranches dotting the area. Clay followed grimly, pushing on as fast as he was able, picking out the faint tracks where they showed and occasionally looking ahead to judge their general direction. From time to time he glanced along his back trail, watching for pursuit, for he knew now that he had a number of hitherto unknown enemies in Pine Flats. He mused on the trouble he had received from Steve Garrett, and could only wonder where the freighter fitted into the scheme of things.

When he reached a small fir-studded knoll he reined into its cover, stood up on his saddle and shinned up a tree. He clung to a substantial bough and peered northwards in the general direction being taken by Cade and Sue, and disappointment filtered into him when he failed to spot movement anywhere. He knew his quarry could not be too far ahead. But the ground was broken and rough, with brush-choked draws and gullies abounding which could easily conceal two riders.

He descended the tree, swung into his saddle to continue, and when he was sure of his direction, sent the sorrel along at a fast clip. He had traversed little more than a mile when he saw where the tracks descended into a draw that led upwards into higher ground. He reined in to study the lie of the land, and decided to remain out of the draw to make better time. He went on along the rim, intent on the chokeberry thickets that grew in profusion in the defile. He could see where horses had forced their way through thicker clumps, and pushed on grimly.

The draw flattened out near the ridge above the long slope, and Clay reined in finally and gazed out over a series of smaller grass-covered ridges beyond which the Bar O was situated. He scanned the rough ground with narrowed gaze, looking for any kind of movement, and was about to ride on when two riders appeared on a crest about one mile ahead. They passed on out of sight so quickly that Clay wondered if he had imagined them, but he set spurs to the sorrel and hammered on in pursuit, pushed by his fears for Sue's safety.

It seemed like ages before he reached the spot where he had seen the riders, and stood up in his stirrups to peer further ahead. The riders were angling left as if heading for the deserted Bar O. Clay recognized Sue instantly, and gazed at the bigger figure of Mike Cade, promising himself a grim accounting when he caught up with them. He waited until there was no chance of being spotted by Cade before going on again, and played a cat and mouse game all the way to the Bar O, staying out of sight as he drew ever closer to his quarry.

Clay watched Cade from the cover of a stand of trees as the man led Sue into the lonely ranch with its burned-out house and the black ground of the recent grass fire surrounding the home area. The barn had escaped the conflagration. He waited impatiently while Cade led the two horses into the barn and closed the door. As soon as there was no chance of being spotted, Clay rode in a wide circle around the spread and fetched up in cover just out of earshot.

He checked his pistol, and kept it in his hand as he walked close to the rear wall of the barn. He was filled with a mingling of deep anger and excitement. No sounds emanated from inside the building when he pressed an ear against the sun-warped boards, and he moved along the rear until he found a convenient knot-hole which provided him with a restricted view of the interior of the building.

Sue was seated on a bale of straw just inside the big front door, bound hand and foot. Cade was standing over her. Clay could hear Sue complaining and protesting about the treatment she was receiving and Cade replied in a low tone which Clay found impossible to decipher. Clay moved around the barn and took up a position by the front door. He cocked his pistol, grasped the handle of the door, and dragged it open to lunge inside.

Clay's sudden appearance shocked Cade, who instinctively dropped a hand to his holstered pistol, but he stopped the movement when he saw Clay's levelled gun. Clay went forward quickly, pistol jutting from his hand. He swung his left fist when he was within an arm's length of Cade and his heavy knuckles smacked solidly against Cade's chin. Cade uttered a cry and fell backwards to lie stretched out on the hard ground with his eyes closed.

Sue looked up at Clay as if she could not believe his appearance. Clay bent over and removed the Colt from Cade's holster before lifting the small hide-out gun from the man's jacket pocket. He slid the derringer into his own pocket before holstering his pistol and untying Sue. The girl threw herself into his arms and clung to him in overwhelming relief.

'Did he hurt you, Sue?' Clay demanded, holding her at arm's length to look into her face. He saw a dull bruise on her cheek and his rising anger sent a flame through him.

'He hit me a couple of times,' Sue admitted, 'and talked of killing me because I refused to marry him. He proposed to me at the FT this morning after you left, and was stung because I told him I'd rather marry my horse! He turned nasty so I decided to stay in town for a few days to keep out of his way, but met him as I approached Pine

Flats, and he forced me to ride with him.'

'Walt Massey saw him hit you and take you along with him. That's how come I'm here now.' Clay turned to Cade and saw his eyes snap shut. He heaved a sigh and bent to secure a hold on Cade's jacket; lifted him bodily from the ground. Cade opened his eyes and Clay released him and stepped back a pace.

'Put up your hands,' Clay rasped. 'You're in for the beating of your life, Cade. I don't expect to be able to knock any sense into you but I'll get a lot of satisfaction from trying.'

'I won't fight you,' Cade replied, shaking his head.

'That don't make no never mind! What was going on in town? Why did you visit Steve Garrett?'

'Who is Steve Garrett?' Cade grimaced. 'I've never heard of him.'

'I saw you go into his office, and when I followed there was no sign of you and Garrett attacked me. It turned into a shoot-out with Garrett and two of his men — Santee and Moore. I had to kill Santee, and then I killed Toomey, who is one of your men. I saw you visit Toomey and Martin at the FT line camp and heard you giving orders to them. So what gives, Cade? What are you after?'

Cade shook his head. There was real fear in his eyes. He slid his right hand around to the back of his belt, and when he brought it back into view he was grasping a knife. Clay fended off the first murderous thrust as the blade darted in for his stomach. His raised left forearm blocked Cade's arm and deflected the blow. Cade whipped his hand back to launch a second attack but Clay's right fist whirled in to deliver a hammering punch that smacked solidly against Cade's chin.

Clay followed up quickly, grasping Cade's wrist as the knife came in to strike him. He twisted Cade's arm sharply and then punched Cade's right bicep with numbing force. The knife clattered on the ground. Clay swung his fist again and connected with Cade's chin a second time. The blow threw Cade over backwards and he fell to the floor and lay on his back. Clay stood over him.

'Come on,' Clay rasped. 'Get up. We've got a lot to settle, Cade, and when I get through with you I'll see to it that you hightail it out of the county. You've pulled your last trick around here. If I catch sight of you again in this neck of the woods I'll kill you.'

Cade did not reply. Clay bent, grasped him and dragged him upright. Cade sagged against Clay's arm, but suddenly became animated with desperate strength and attempted to smash his forehead into Clay's face in a vicious butt. But he was not tall enough to deliver a telling blow. He merely grazed Clay's chin as Clay pulled back to avoid the blow.

Cade grasped Clay around the neck and attempted to throttle him. Clay struck shrewdly with a rib-cracking blow that doubled up the slighter man and dumped him back on the ground. Clay's simmering anger finally burst through his control and he dragged Cade upright to attack him with both fists. Cade took half-a-dozen solid blows to the body before he went down yet again; this time he was out cold.

Clay stood over Cade; fists clenched. A burning anger flared in his mind. Cade lay motionless with his arms outflung. His face was bruised and blood was seeping from his nostrils. He was gasping for air, his chest rising and falling laboriously. Clay unclenched his hands. He glanced at Sue, who was standing in the background, a hand to her mouth and her expressive face pale with shock.

'I haven't finished with him yet,' Clay said harshly. 'I've got a lot of questions in my mind that only he can answer. But I'd better take you back to FT. It's not safe for you to ride alone while this trouble is going on. There's no telling who is mixed up in it. My father is lying wounded in Doc Miller's house, and it seems Snape Ritter is involved somehow. He sent two killers into town to finish off Pa, but I was lucky enough to stop them.'

Sue opened her mouth to reply but was distracted by a sound at the door and glanced over her shoulder. Clay shifted his gaze and saw Sim Martin stepping into view with a levelled pistol in his right hand.

'Looks like I got here just in time,' Martin said with a grin. 'Just try and reach for your gun, mister. I owe you for killing Shorty Allen.'

Clay lifted his hands clear of his waist and tensed his muscles in anticipation of attacking Martin should the opportunity arise. But the gunman was well versed in the grim art of handling this kind of situation and stayed out of arm's length.

'Go round the back of the big feller and take his gun out of its holster,' Martin ordered Sue. 'Don't get between him and me. I ain't bothered about shooting a woman, so I'll drop you pretty quick if I have to. We're playing for keeps now.'

'Do as he says, Sue,' Clay advised, raising his hands shoulder high. 'He's one of three gunnies Cade brought in to cause trouble, and I've killed two of them.'

'Is Toomey dead?' Martin demanded. 'He went into Garrett's office ahead of me and I heard a shot as I left.'

'I beat him to the shot,' Clay said.

'So that's another one I owe you. We'll see what Cade wants done with you before I gut-shoot you, mister. You sure are hell on wheels, huh? And Cade reckoned this job would be a push-over. He sure pegged you wrong. Get on with it, lady. Take his gun and throw it on the ground.'

Sue walked around Clay, drew his pistol and tossed it to one side. Clay expelled his pent-up breath in a long sigh. His eyes glittered as he watched Martin, who was glancing at the motionless Cade.

'He ain't gonna be too happy when he wakes up,' Martin observed. 'What goes on between you two?'

'It goes back a long way,' Clay said, 'but it's coming to an end now.'

'Yeah, and you are grasping the dirty end of the stick!' Martin grinned. 'Get that piece of rope on the floor, gal, and tie his hands behind his back. Do a good job because I'll check the knots.'

Clay put his hands behind his back and Sue bound his wrists together with the rope Cade had used to bind her. Martin checked the knots and grunted in satisfaction.

'Now both of you sit on that bale of straw and stay still while I take a look at Cade.' Martin waggled his gun. 'Just remember I'm hoping for an excuse to plug you, mister,' he added.

Clay lowered himself on to the bale and Sue sat down beside him. They watched Martin drop to one knee beside the prostrate Cade and begin to revive him. Cade stirred and opened his eyes. Clay leaned sideways to Sue and whispered urgently in her ear.

'Cade's hide-out gun is in my pocket,' he hissed. 'Take it out and shoot Martin.'

Sue glanced up into his face with horror dawning in her eyes.

'Do it,' Clay urged. 'They'll kill both of us if you don't. Be quick, Sue.'

'Quit talking,' Martin rapped. 'We'll get to you in a minute.'

He began to pull Cade to his feet. At first he had to support Cade, but the man slowly recovered and eventually stood alone. He was severely shaken by the beating he had taken and was unsteady, his mouth agape, his breathing erratic and his hands trembling. Clay watched him intently.

'You've beaten me for the last time, Overman,' Cade rasped. 'Now you've reached the end of your rope. I waited years to come back to Pine Flats and repay you for the way you beat me when I was a kid.'

He staggered then, almost fell, and turned to walk unsteadily to the door of the barn where he leaned against a post for support.

'Are you OK?' Martin demanded. 'You look like you've been flattened in a stampede. What do you want me to do with these two?'

'I'm gonna ride to FT,' Cade said, lowering his head and closing his eyes. 'Get my horse and help me into the saddle. You stay here and kill these two when I've ridden out. Then go back to town and finish off Pete Overman. He's lying up at the doctor's house. When you've done that go see Steve Garrett to ask if there's anything he needs handling.'

'Sure,' Martin said, grinning.

Clay watched intently as Martin fetched Cade's horse to the doorway and then helped the man into his saddle. Cade sat slumped, one hand resting on the saddle horn. He swayed as Martin slapped the horse across its rump and started out of the doorway.

'Be quick, Sue,' Clay said desperately as Cade disappeared from view. 'Get the gun out of my pocket before Martin turns on us. He'll kill us for sure if you don't stop him.'

Sue expelled her breath in a heavy sigh and reached into Clay's pocket. Her trembling fingers closed around the butt of the small two-shot gun and she drew it slowly, gasping in shock as tension gripped her.

Martin had placed his pistol on the ground while he helped Cade and it was lying several yards from where he was standing. He glanced in their direction as he turned in the doorway, saw Sue lifting the gun clear of Clay's pocket, and uttered a shout as he dived for his gun.

'Shoot him, Sue!' Clay rasped.

Sue cocked the gun as Martin dropped to his knees and scooped up his pistol. Sue covered him with the derringer as he spun around, his pistol lifting. She clenched her teeth and squeezed the trigger. The report of the shot was loud in the confines of the barn. Martin uttered a cry as the bullet smashed into his chest. His gun spilled from his hand and he twisted sharply to fall upon his face as echoes drifted and faded.

Sue sat motionless, gripped by shock. Clay was sweating in his helplessness.

'Quick, Sue, untie my hands,' he snapped. 'Hurry it up. I want Cade before he can get to FT.'

He struggled to his feet and Sue stepped behind him. She dropped the gun and fumbled with the ropes binding his wrists, but was shaking so badly she could barely use her fingers on the knots. Eventually the rope fell away and Clay heaved a sigh of relief. He ran to where his pistol was lying, snatched it up, and hurried to the doorway of the barn. He shook his head when he looked out and saw Cade riding out of pistol range. He turned to Sue, who was trembling and badly shocked.

'Come on, Sue, we're not out of the woods yet,' he encouraged. 'Get into your saddle. My horse is out back. Let's get moving. I need to nail Cade.'

He ran out of the barn to fetch his horse, but, as he rounded the rear corner he collided with a big figure standing behind it. A fist came out of nowhere and smacked him solidly on the chin. The blow was powerful enough to dump Clay on the seat of his pants, and a black curtain seemed to drop before his eyes. He blinked rapidly but to no avail. Sight and hearing receded and he fell into a deep pit of unconsciousness . . .

The next thing Clay became aware of was a heavy hand slapping his face. He surfaced reluctantly and opened his eyes to find himself gazing into the coarse, fleshy features of Snape Ritter.

'Hey, it was only a little smack,' Ritter said with a grin. 'I thought you were a lot tougher than this, Overman. Now tell me what the hell is going on. I went to FT after our little fracas this morning to pick up a pistol, and I've been out here looking for you ever since. Where have you been skulking?'

Clay struggled to sit up and Ritter snaked Clay's gun out of its holster. He stuck the muzzle into Clay's stomach.

'Get your hands up,' he rasped. 'I'm gonna kill you. With you dead I can go back to Pine Flats.'

'You'll make the biggest mistake of your life if you ride into town,' Clay advised him. 'While you've been hiding yourself out on the range I've been in Pine Flats handling the trouble that's come up, and there was hell to pay. Several men have been killed, and everyone knows you sent two killers in to murder my father. You've thrown in with Cade and Garrett, Ritter, and it is all out in the open.'

Ritter's mouth gaped and his eyes narrowed.

'Say, what are you giving me?' he demanded. 'If you think you can save yourself by lying then you better think again.'

'You're the one needs to do some thinking,' Clay responded. 'I was in the jail talking to my father when Toomey and Martin turned up to kill him. I shot Shorty Allen, and Toomey was killed in Garrett's office. Martin just cashed in his chips. He's lying in the barn, as you can see for yourself. You don't know it yet, but it is all over for you.'

Ritter shook his head wordlessly, his face revealing shock. He motioned with his pistol.

'Let's take a look in the barn,' he said. 'I don't trust you, Overman, and I ain't taking your word for a damn thing.'

Clay turned, and at that moment Sue appeared around the front corner of the building, mounted on her paint. She reined in when she saw Ritter, and her expression tightened at the sight of the deputy's drawn gun.

'What are you doing here?' Ritter demanded.

'Ask Mike Cade, if you ever see him again,' Clay said. 'Cade showed his hand and he's finished around here. If you've got any sense, Ritter, you'll spread leather and get to hell out. Paul

Edlin sent a man over to Sunset Ridge to fetch Sheriff Cooper. If you're still around when he shows up you'll find yourself behind bars, and they'll throw away the key.'

'I don't believe this.' Ritter shook his head. 'Go back inside the barn. Get off that horse, gal. Cade said you two had to be silenced, and I'll handle that.'

Clay walked ahead of Ritter. Sue slid out of her saddle and led the animal back into the barn. Ritter looked down at the motionless Sim Martin, and heaved a sigh as he met Clay's hard gaze.

'Why did you kill him?' he demanded.

'Clay didn't — I did,' Sue said. 'He was fixing to kill us and I got him first.'

'Jeez, I don't like the sound of this,' Ritter mused. 'I don't like this at all.'

'You better believe it.' Clay was watching Ritter closely, knowing he had little chance of outwitting the deputy. Ritter's pistol was steady in his hand and the muzzle never wavered from Clay's chest. Clay could feel desperation filtering into his mind, and prepared to take any reasonable chance to overpower the crooked deputy.

Sue turned her paint around to face the door. She slapped it hard across the rump as it brushed against Ritter. The highly strung animal reared and swung, almost knocking the deputy off balance. Clay threw himself forward eagerly, hands outstretched to grapple with Ritter, and the next instant he was fighting for his life . . .

9

Clay's outstretched right hand knocked Ritter's pistol aside. He clenched his left hand into a fist and swung it at the deputy's prominent jaw. His knuckles connected as he collided with Ritter and they both fell backwards. Clay kneed Ritter in the stomach and then hit him in the face with his elbow. Ritter yelled in anger and his heavy fists slammed into Clay's body. Clay twisted away and pushed up to his hands and knees. He looked up to see Ritter reaching for his fallen gun, which was lying only inches from his hand and, as Ritter grasped the weapon, Clay dived at him, fists flailing.

They rolled on the dusty floor of the barn, each fighting for supremacy. Clay received a blow to his face that made his left eye water. He blinked and shook his head, and then reached for Ritter's right arm and twisted it, throwing his weight behind the move. Ritter yelled and squirmed away. They parted and got quickly to their feet, breathing heavily. Ritter lifted both hands high in front of his face and began to circle, his face showing intentness. He jabbed out his left fist and Clay avoided it easily as he stepped in and started a quick two-handed attack that drove Ritter back across the barn.

Ritter suddenly tripped and fell heavily, and Clay saw that Sue had thrust the handle of a pitchfork between the deputy's legs to put him down. Ritter landed heavily on his back and Sue stood over him with the tines of the pitchfork pointed ominously at his face.

'Pick up the gun, Clay,' Sue yelled, and Clay turned to snatch up the discarded pistol. He cocked it and covered Ritter, who sat up slowly, his hands still clenched.

'You had enough, huh, Overman?' Ritter demanded. 'Or are you gonna let that gal take over? Put the gun down and get back to fist-fighting.'

'Some other time,' Clay replied. 'I need to see Mike Cade fast, and you'll go with me to FT. So get up and shut up. You're finished, Ritter. I'm taking you to jail.'

'You ain't got no right to jug me, you polecat.' Ritter sneered. 'So how long have you been wearing a star? Come on, let's get back to fighting.'

Clay waggled the gun. 'I told you to shut up,' he said firmly. 'Where's your horse?'

'Go find it,' the deputy snarled. 'I ain't telling you a thing.'

'That's OK by me!' Clay grimaced. 'You can walk to FT and then all the way back to town. I'll rope and drag you like a fat hog. Now get up and start moving. You've got a long hike ahead of you.'

Ritter scowled and got to his feet. Clay backed off, keeping out of reach, only too aware of Ritter's trickery when it came to fighting. Sue grasped her paint's bridle and led the horse out of the barn. She bent and picked up Cade's hideout gun, which was lying just inside the barn, and slipped it into her pocket. Clay motioned for Ritter to precede him and they went out into the yard.

'My horse is back of the barn,' Ritter said grudgingly.

'So you don't fancy walking, huh?' Clay followed the deputy around to the back of the barn and saw Ritter's grey standing with trailing reins. He went to the animal and searched the saddle-bags, found a pair of handcuffs, and tossed them to Ritter. 'Put a cuff on your left wrist,' he instructed, 'then stick your hands behind your back. I'm not taking any chances with you.'

Ritter snapped a cuff around his left wrist and turned his back as he thrust his hands behind him. Clay stepped in, held his gun against Ritter's spine, and used his left hand to snap the right cuff into place. He holstered his gun, grabbed Ritter, and thrust him up into his saddle. Sue went for Clay's sorrel and led the animal back to the barn.

Clay swung into his saddle and took hold of Ritter's reins.

'OK let's go,' he said, and touched spurs to his animal's flanks.

They rode out for the FT ranch. Cade was long gone now, and Clay gazed around uneasily, his mind leaping ahead as he tried to plan his actions for when they arrived at the ranch. He led Ritter's grey by the reins, and kept glancing back at the sullen deputy as they progressed. Sue rode slightly behind them, and when she caught Clay's glance at her she smiled wanly in response. Clay could see that she was badly shocked and beckoned her to ride beside him.

'Are you OK, Sue?' he asked solicitously. 'You're looking a bit peaky right now.'

'I'm gonna have nightmares about killing Martin,' she replied, 'and nothing you can say will alter that. Just let it lie and give me time to come to terms with it, huh?'

'All I want to say is that when you see him in your dreams, lying dead in the barn, just tell yourself that if you hadn't killed him then it would be the two of us lying there in his place. Will you do that?'

'I promise to try it,' Sue replied wearily.

Clay sighed and looked ahead. They would soon sight the FT ranch house, and relief filled him as they rode nearer. He had no doubt what would happen when Big Frank learned the facts of Cade's duplicity. The rancher would take up a gun and there would an end to the trouble Cade had caused.

The sound of shooting at the ranch sent echoes across the range and Clay reined in abruptly when he heard it. Several more shots hammered as Clay gazed enquiringly at Sue. Clay recovered from his surprise and threw down Ritter's reins.

'Stay here, Sue,' he rasped. 'I'll ride

ahead and see what's going on. Keep an eye on Ritter. Don't let him ride off.'

He sent the sorrel forward at a run and, when he glanced back over his shoulder, he saw Sue producing a gun and covering Ritter. He slowed when he could see the ranch yard, and his eyes turned bleak at the sight of three bodies sprawled in the dust. Four other men were down in cover, facing the house. A shot was fired from the open front doorway on the porch and the four men replied. Gunsmoke drifted across the yard and sullen echoes fled across the illimitable range.

Clay dismounted in cover and tied the reins of his sorrel to a nearby branch. He drew his pistol and checked it before moving forward to assess the situation. When he saw that one of the men attacking the ranch house was Payne, the ranch foreman, he paused in shock.

The gun in the doorway of the house spurted smoke again and dust flew up from the ground in front of Payne's big figure. Clay saw someone peering around the door post of the house and recognized Big Frank Truscott. The rancher called out, his voice ringing through the dying gun echoes.

'Come on, you buzzards. Come and take me if you can. There's plenty of fight in me. If you want this spread, Payne, then you'll have to grab it the hard way.'

Payne reared up and loosed two quick shots at the doorway. Clay saw splinters fly from close to Big Frank's head. He started forward, gun ready, wondering what was going on. He looked more closely at the three men with Payne and recognized them as regular FT crew. So what were they doing shooting at their boss?

Clay paused and then turned and hunted cover. He ran in a wide circle around the yard, keeping out of sight of the foreman, and made for the rear of the house. When he could see the kitchen door he dropped into cover and looked around but saw no sign of

190

anyone watching the back. He got up and went in closer. The kitchen door was unlocked and he entered, closing the door at his back. He called loudly to attract Big Frank's attention as he walked through to the front living-room. Gunsmoke was drifting through the lower rooms.

'Hey, Frank, hold your fire,' Clay called. 'This is Clay Overman. What's going on?'

For a moment there was no response, and then Big Frank replied.

'Come on through, Clay, but keep your head down. I got some polecat trouble, and you're just in time to give me a hand.'

Clay entered the front room. Big Frank was on one knee just inside the open door. He was reloading his pistol. There was blood on his shirt which had trickled down from a cut on his forehead. He grinned at Clay.

'Where in hell did you come from, Clay? I'm sure glad to see you.'

'So what's happening?' Clay demanded.

'That damn Mike Cade rode in some time ago looking like he'd come off second best in a fight with a wildcat. He had a few words with Payne, grabbed a fresh horse, and rode straight out again. When he'd gone the shooting started. I don't know what got into Payne. He called out three of the crew and they joined him in shooting at me. I sure wish I knew what this is all about.'

Clay moved into a position from which he could view the yard. Payne reared up and fired two shots at him. The bullets slammed into the wood-work of the door and Clay ducked.

'They sure are playing for keeps,' Clay observed.

'Are any of them out back?' Big Frank demanded.

'I didn't see any, but they could get wise and move around to cut us off.' Clay cocked his gun and watched for movement out front. 'I've got Ritter handcuffed out there. He's mixed up in this trouble. Sue is with him. I think we'd better get out of here, Frank. We should get your horse and make for town.'

'I ain't going anywhere unless they carry me out feet first,' Big Frank replied pugnaciously. 'This is my spread and no one is gonna run me out. I don't know the half of what is going on, but I'll fight to the last shot to keep what is mine. You go on back to Sue and take her to town, Clay. I want her safe. I can handle this bunch of pack rats.'

Clay was aware that he would be unable to dissuade Big Frank from his present frame of mind, and he was torn between his concern for the rancher and fears for Sue's safety. Cade was still out there somewhere, running loose and ready to kill for whatever it was he wanted. He ducked when a bullet smacked into the door post close to his head, threw up his pistol and snapped off two shots at a head and arm which showed briefly from behind the water trough over by the corral.

'Throw down your gun and come on out, Frank,' Payne yelled. 'You ain't got a prayer. Cut your losses and give up.'

'You reckon to take over FT, huh?' Big Frank responded. 'You already own a quarter-share of the spread, Payne. Ain't that enough for you?'

'It is nothing personal,' Payne replied. 'I was pushed into this. Blood is thicker than water, Frank, and I've got to go along with Mike. He's my sister's boy, and has been planning this for a long time. So come on out.'

'Like hell I will!' Frank reared up and emptied his pistol at Payne. Then he ducked and reloaded his spent chambers.

Clay wrinkled his nose at the acrid smell of cordite. He lifted his gun, looking for the chance to hit the gunmen, but Payne had disappeared into cover.

'I'll go out and sneak around them,' Clay said. 'Don't shoot me by mistake.'

'I've told you what to do,' Big Frank replied. 'Just get Sue and take her out of this. I'll come into town when I've put Payne down in the dust. I'm gonna fire the whole dang crew and hire a new outfit. Half those men out there I called my friends, and now they are shooting at me. Go on, Clay, clear out of here. What I've got to do ain't pretty, not by a long rope.'

Clay eased back from the doorway and departed quickly. He had no clear idea of what he should do, but Sue had to take priority in his plans. He paused just inside the kitchen door and peered out the window, ducking back when he saw one of the crew approaching with a pistol in his hand. He stepped behind the door and flattened against the wall. The next instant the door was thrust open. Clay leaned forward as the cowboy entered, and jabbed him with the muzzle of his gun.

'I got you dead to rights, Curly,' Clay rasped. 'Drop the gun and put your hands up.'

Curly froze, released his gun and it thudded on the floor.

'So what's going on?' Clay demanded. 'How come you and the others are shooting at Big Frank?'

'You'll have to talk to Payne about that,' Curly replied. 'I'm just following orders.'

'What are Payne's orders? I thought Big Frank was the boss around here.'

'Not any more he ain't. Payne bought him out, so he says, but Big Frank changed his mind and won't quit. We're kind of trying to get him to go quietly.'

'Do you expect me to believe that? Go into the storeroom and close the door. I'll lock you in and you can stay there while I talk to Payne. I need to find out what is going on.'

Curly shrugged and crossed the kitchen. He entered the storeroom and closed the door. Clay followed closely and pushed home the bolt. He picked up the puncher's discarded gun, stuck it into his waistband, and then left the kitchen to walk quickly from the rear of the house to hunt cover. He checked the loads in his pistol before moving on to circle the yard.

Clay eased in behind the shack where Payne lived. He peered through a small back window, saw the place was empty, and moved around to the front corner. Payne was entering the barn. Clay moved in, keeping the shack between him and the barn. Two of the outfit were still shooting at the front doorway of the house, and Big Frank was snapping shots in return. Clay went to the rear of the barn and sneaked in through the back door.

Payne was saddling his black horse. Clay went forward, his gun steady in his hand. He glanced around and saw the barn was otherwise deserted.

'OK, Payne,' he rasped. 'Throw up your hands. Don't turn around.'

The ranch foreman froze at the sound of Clay's voice and all movement ceased. He raised his hands slowly and Clay went forward to snatch Payne's gun from its holster.

'So what is this all about?' Clay demanded. 'How come you've thrown in with Cade? I had you pegged for an honest man. How did Cade get to you?'

'I never got a fair deal off Big Frank,' Payne grated, 'and when Mike came up with a scheme I went along with it.'

'Maybe you have got a grievance against Frank, but what about Big O?' Clay demanded. 'Pa and me, we never upset anyone. We always minded our own business and lived within the law. So how did we get dragged into this? We've been burned out, and there was hell to pay in Pine Flats today.'

Payne glanced over his shoulder at Clay. Desperation showed in his expression.

'I'm going back to town shortly,' Clay said, 'and I'll take you along. I'll put you in jail until the sheriff shows up.'

'You've got no right to stick your nose into this,' Payne said harshly. He whirled around as Clay stepped back, and his outstretched right hand struck Clay's gun hand and knocked it aside. 'You ain't taking me anywhere,' he rasped, and crashed his right fist against Clay's jaw.

It seemed to Clay as if the barn had fallen in on him. The blow almost dropped him to his knees. He dimly felt his pistol being snatched from his hand and hurled himself at Payne, his arms encircling the big foreman to prevent him using the gun. Payne slammed his right knee into Clay's groin. Clay threw himself backwards and landed on his back with Payne hugged to him in a desperate embrace.

Clay's sight cleared and he swung his left fist in a short punch that smacked against Payne's chin. The foreman grunted and redoubled his efforts to bring the muzzle of the pistol he was holding to line up on Clay's chest. Clay used his head in a powerful butt, smashing his forehead into Payne's face. Blood spurted from Payne's nose and he tried to break Clay's grip but Clay clung to him and struck again with his head.

They fell apart and both men started

to their feet. Payne had lost the gun and lunged at Clay with an upraised boot. Clay dived forward and his arms encircled the foreman's legs just above the knees. Payne fell like a cottonwood struck by lightning and Clay pushed himself upright and swung his right fist in a series of telling blows that stretched Payne out senseless.

Clay picked up his gun. He stood over Payne, saw the foreman was out, and took a lariat from the black's saddle horn. By the time Payne opened his eyes he was trussed and helpless. Clay left the foreman lying where he was and went to the front door of the barn. He looked out and saw three men walking towards the porch of the ranch house with guns in their hands. He spotted Big Frank lying motionless in the doorway of the house, his gun discarded.

Clay fired a shot over the heads of the three 'punchers and they jerked around to face him. He cocked his pistol as he called out.

'I've got Payne hogtied in here and it looks to me like the trouble is over now, so anyone ranged against Big Frank had better pull stakes and get the hell out.'

'We ain't going anywhere,' one of the men replied, and lifted his gun to start shooting.

Hot lead flew around Clay and he jumped back into the barn. He peered across the yard and saw the three 'punchers turn to stalk him. He clenched his teeth, holstered his gun, and grabbed the reins of Payne's black. Bullets smashed into the front door of the barn and the crash of shots echoed raucously. Clay led the black out the back door, sprang into the saddle, and set off for the spot where he had left Sue.

He was not pursued and quickly reached the cover where he had last seen Sue. He reined in and looked around anxiously for she was nowhere to be seen. Ritter was sitting his saddle, his hands still cuffed behind his back, and Sue had tied the crooked deputy's reins to the branch of a tree.

'Where's Sue?' Clay demanded.

'Why ask me?' Ritter countered angrily. 'She took off the minute you went into the yard. She's gonna get herself into a heap of trouble before she's through, you mark my words.'

'Which way did she ride?' Clay demanded.

Ritter grinned as he jerked his head in the general direction of the ranch and his dark eyes filled with a malicious gleam. 'Right now she'll be in Cade's hands again, I shouldn't wonder, and that's the last thing you want, huh?'

Clay uttered an imprecation as he pulled the black around and spurred back to the ranch. He drew his pistol and urged the horse on, following the well-worn trail into the yard but he reined in quickly when he saw Sue on the porch with two of the three 'punchers who had been shooting at Big Frank. The third man appeared in the doorway of the barn when he heard the sound of the black's hoofs, and

Payne showed himself at the man's shoulder with a gun in his hand. Clay hauled on the reins and turned the black quickly to ride back out of sight, as both men opened fire, and he retreated in a hail of flying lead.

10

Clay swung the black to the right and rode in a circle back to the rear door of the barn. Gun in hand, he entered the barn and dived out of the saddle, gun lifting to trade lead, but Payne was already on his way across the yard. Clay ran forward to the front door of the barn, fired a shot over the foreman's head, and Payne whirled and dropped to one knee in the dust, the pistol in his hand lifting.

'Throw down your gun, Payne,' Clay yelled, taking aim at the foreman. 'I'll kill you if you try anything. I want Sue out of there now. Throw down your gun or you're dead.'

'You can't fight all of us,' Payne replied, 'and if you try then Sue is likely to get hurt. You throw down your gun and come on out. There's nothing you can do now.'

Clay clenched his teeth and aimed his pistol at Payne's right shoulder. He squeezed the trigger and the weapon kicked against the heel of his hand. Payne yelled in agony when the slug hit him. He was thrown half around by the half-inch chunk of lead and fell backwards as if his legs had been kicked from under him.

'I'm not playing games,' Clay yelled through the echoes of the shot, 'and there's plenty more of that if you want it.'

The 'puncher with Payne threw down his gun and raised his hands. He was standing in the open and had nowhere to hide. Clay looked at the house and saw the two men on the porch pushing Sue into the house and following her closely. One of them dragged Big Frank out of the doorway before the door was slammed. Clay lowered his gun. It looked like a stand-off, and he called to the 'puncher standing beside Payne.

'Come on back to the barn and make it quick.'

The man hesitated, but with Clay's gun menacing him he had no alternative but to obey the command. He kept his hands shoulder-high as he approached. Clay studied his face closely, but did not recognize him as one of the regular outfit. The man paused before Clay, his face sullen.

'You're not one of the regular FT riders,' Clay said.

'No,' the man replied grudgingly. 'Four of us came from Kansas, where we knew Mike Cade. He offered us work so here we are.'

'Gun work and hell-raising, huh?' Clay's expression was hard. 'Well, that's come to an end today. Where is Cade now?'

'He came in a short while ago, changed horses and rode off back to town. He said something about looking up a man called Clay Overman.'

'I'm Overman, and he won't want to find me in town, but I'll ride back there and look him up. Is Big Frank dead?'

'Not yet, but he looks bad. So you're

Clay Overman!'

'That's what my mother called me! Get down on your knees.'

The man's expression changed as he obeyed. Clay stepped behind him, pushed off his Stetson with his left hand, and struck hard with his levelled Colt. The man groaned as the long barrel crashed against his skull and he fell forward on his face. Clay looked around the barn for some rope, picked up Payne's lariat, and quickly bound the unconscious man. He went to the front door and peered out across the yard.

Payne was crawling towards the house. Blood was dribbling from his shoulder.

'Hold it, Payne,' Clay called. 'I got you covered, and you ain't going anywhere. I need you as an ace in the hole when I go for Cade, but first we're gonna get Sue out of the house. Stand up and take what's coming to you. Do like I say or you're dead, mister.'

Payne glanced back at Clay, saw the

levelled gun covering him, and slumped on to his face and lay motionless. Clay expelled his pent up breath in a long sigh and looked ahead at the ranch house. He could see a harsh face at one of the front windows and an uplifted gun ready to trade lead. He clenched his teeth in frustration. He did not think the two men in the house would harm Sue, but could not risk the girl's life by pushing the situation.

'Tell those men in the house to turn Sue loose,' Clay rasped.

'Not a chance,' Payne growled. 'She's got to die the same as Big Frank. You know we can't let them live.'

'You don't have a choice, Payne. Do like I say or I'll kill you.'

'Go to hell!' Payne's pale face took on a dogged expression. He looked up at Clay and grinned. 'You can't win this, and you better quit while you're ahead.'

Clay aimed at Payne's right leg and fired. The foreman's limb jerked as the slug hit him, and he yelled in agony. He grasped his leg above the knee.

'You're a crazy son of a bitch!' Payne yelled.

'Call Sue out or you'll get a slug in your other leg. And if that doesn't make up your mind for you then I'll start in on your arms. Get to it, Payne.'

Payne gazed at Clay for a moment, shaking his head in disbelief. Clay raised the pistol again and drew a bead on the foreman's left leg.

'Hold it,' Payne yelled. 'I'll do like you say.' He looked towards the house. 'Hey, Thompson, send the girl out.'

Clay waited, gun upraised. For a couple of moments there was no reaction from the house, and then the door opened slowly and Sue appeared on the porch.

'Over here, Sue,' Clay called.

The girl stepped off the porch and came across the yard. Her face was set stiffly in shock. She passed Payne without so much as a glance at him, and when she reached Clay he grasped her arm and pulled her into the shelter of the barn.

'Let's get out of here,' Clay said urgently.

'I can't leave!' she protested. 'My father is badly wounded.'

'So let's head back to town and get the doc out here. You can't help Big Frank by remaining, and Cade will have you shot if you stick around.'

'I won't go,' Sue said stubbornly. 'Please don't make me, Clay.'

Clay studied her taut features for a moment, his mind ticking over as he reviewed the situation.

'OK,' he said at length. 'Let's try something else. You get in the black's saddle and ride out. Watch what happens from a distance while I try to get those two men out of the house. If I succeed then we'll attend to Big Frank, but if I fail then you hightail it to town and get the doc and some of the townsmen out here. Go on, get moving. While you're in Payne's hands I can't win, so give me a chance to beat this setup.'

'I'll wait here while you do what you

have to,' Sue replied doggedly.

Clay looked into her face while he considered, and then turned his attention to Payne.

'One thing more, Payne,' he called. 'I want those two men out of the house so give them a shout. They are to come out unarmed and with their hands up.'

Payne stirred himself. He shook his head.

'You're overplaying your hand,' he replied. 'I got rid of the men on the payroll who were loyal to Big Frank and replaced them with my own men. Some more of them will be riding in pretty soon, and if they catch you here you'll be done for. Why don't you get out while you've still got a chance?'

'No dice! I'm in this to the end. Do like I say or I'll put another slug in you.'

Payne looked towards the house and yelled in an echoing voice for the men to show themselves. After a moment the front door opened a fraction and the muzzle of a pistol appeared. Two shots were fired and dust spurted up in the yard a foot to Payne's left.

'There's your answer,' Payne remarked when the gun echoes had died away. 'It's out of my hands now.'

Clay lifted his gun and then lowered it. He knew when he was beaten. He turned to Sue and reached out to grasp her arm.

'We've got to get out of here,' he said sharply. 'Let's head for town and get the doc.'

Sue shook her head. Clay turned his head when he caught the sound of approaching hoofs and spotted four riders coming along the trail from Pine Flats. His teeth clicked together when he recognized Steve Garrett in the lead.

'We've run out of time,' he said tersely, and hurried Sue to where Payne's black was standing. He thrust the girl unceremoniously into the saddle and slapped the animal's rump.

'Head for town and get help,' he called, as the horse lunged forward and started running. 'I'll stay between you and these men as long as I can.'

He turned back to the yard when the black disappeared from sight and levelled his gun. Garrett and his men had reined in at the front edge of the yard and Garrett called to Payne.

'What in hell is going on, Payne?' the freighter demanded. 'Where's Clay Overman?'

'I'm here, Garrett,' Clay replied, and fired a shot which struck the ground a scant inch from the right foreleg of Garrett's horse. The animal cavorted nervously and Garrett almost fell out of his saddle. He reined about and sought cover, taking his companions with him.

Clay fired two more shots, before turning and making for the back door of the barn. He ran for cover out back and angled to the left, heading for the spot where he had left Ritter hand-cuffed. He ducked into the shelter of a stand of trees just outside the yard and watched while Garrett led his men forward on foot to take over the yard. He was able to hear their excited voices when Garrett questioned Payne. When the freighter's gun help fanned out to search the ranch, Clay continued on his way.

Ritter was still sitting helpless in his saddle when Clay reached the deputy. He grabbed the crooked lawman and dragged him out of the saddle.

'What's going on?' Ritter demanded as Clay mounted the horse. 'Are you adding horse-stealing to your other crimes?' His expression changed when Clay turned the horse to ride away. 'Hey, you can't leave me here,' he yelled in fury.

Clay rode out with Ritter's angry voice cutting at him as he departed. He rode into the nearest cover and kept going until he was clear of the ranch before swinging in a wide circle to head for town. When he reached a knoll he reined in and looked ahead, pleased to see Sue in the distance, riding hell for leather to Pine Flats. He prepared to ride after the girl, but a bullet snarled in his right ear and he looked back over his shoulder to see three riders bearing down on him from the direction of the ranch.

It hadn't taken Garrett long to organize a pursuit, Clay thought, as he dug his heels into the flanks of the horse. He rode into cover and turned to fight, determined to buy Sue all the time she might need to fetch help. He dragged his Winchester from its boot and stepped down from the saddle, trailed his reins and moved away from the horse. He waited stoically for the riders to draw within range, and then started shooting, and the trio turned aside and sought cover from his questing lead.

Clay returned to the horse, mounted and rode on, making for another crest, and when he turned at bay once more he found only two riders on his tail. A flurry of well-aimed shots turned them back and he continued. As he topped a rise about four miles from Pine Flats he was startled by the appearance of a rider coming towards him. His rifle lifted but he stayed the movement when he recognized Sue.

'What in Sam Hill are you doing here?' he demanded. 'You should have reached town by now.'

'I heard shooting on my back trail and thought you were in bad trouble.'

'I was holding off pursuit. While I was shooting you should have realized that I was still in action. Now get out of here, Sue. You need to get the doctor started for FT to take care of Big Frank.'

Sue turned her horse and rode back the way she had come. Clay watched her for a moment, and then glanced along his back trail. He didn't know whether to be pleased or anxious when he failed to spot movement back there, but he believed the bad men would not call off their attempts to finish him.

He dismounted and checked his weapons before stretching out behind a crest and waiting for trouble to come up to him. The sun was blazing down, making him feel hot and uncomfortable. He cuffed sweat from his brow and narrowed his eyes against the glare as he watched for trouble. When a bullet whined over his head, coming from his right, he guessed his pursuers had circled around him, and prepared to fight. A rifle fired a stream of lead at his position to keep his head down, and he rolled away and dropped into a slight depression. When he lifted his head to look around he saw a rider coming at him from his left, and discouraged the man with some accurate shooting.

The gunfight lasted until Clay put a slug in the man coming from the left. Then the shooting stopped and echoes fled suddenly. The man on the right pulled out a few moments later. Clay saw him riding down a slope more than a hundred yards away to vanish in some brush in a draw. Minutes later he reappeared higher up the slope and disappeared over the crest.

Clay remained where he was, listening to the heavy silence which ensued. He could see the man on the left lying unmoving on the ground; his horse cropping grass nearby. A growing weakness invaded Clay's body and he lay with his head on his arms, waiting for the bad feeling to pass. He became aware that he was desperately thirsty, and could not remember when he had eaten his last meal. He pushed himself up on to his knees to check his surroundings.

He lurched to his feet and staggered to where Ritter's horse stood with trailing reins. He checked for ammunition and discovered he was getting short of pistol cartridges. But he had Ritter's pistol in his waistband and found five shells in its cylinder. He rode out towards Pine Flats, his Stetson pulled low over his eyes. The sun was well over in the western half of the sky now and night would not come soon enough.

Clay could see the roofs of the town in the background when he reined in to watch half-a-dozen riders coming towards him. Sue was leading them,

218

and he relaxed somewhat when he saw Doc Miller beside the girl. As they drew nearer he recognized more faces, and knew these were some of the regular posse men from Pine Flats. They came up fast and reined in about him, asking questions which he did not attempt to answer.

'Where's Edlin?' Clay demanded. 'He's the only lawman we've got. Did Sue tell you about Ritter?'

'Edlin is sticking around town,' Doc Miller replied. 'He won't leave the jail. He put your pa back behind bars, Clay, and says he'll hold him until the sheriff shows up. He reckons Pete will be a whole lot safer under lock and key. Jake Moore tried to kill your pa at my place. And Walt Massey was found dead in the stable after you rode out.'

'Massey is dead?' Clay shook his head. 'Did Sue tell you about Cade and Payne, and Ritter?'

'I've been explaining what happened to us while we were riding,' Sue cut in. 'Can we go on, please? My father could be dying for want of attention while we sit around here jawing.'

'Sure.' Doc Miller seemed to be in charge of the law party. He touched spurs to his horse and rode on, taking the posse with him.

Sue looked closely at Clay. 'You look like all hell,' she observed. 'You'd better go on to town and take care of yourself. Make sure Pete is OK. I'll see you later, huh?'

Clay nodded and Sue went on, spurring her paint to catch up with the doctor. Clay watched them until they were out of sight, before he continued to Pine Flats.

The main street was deserted and silent when Clay rode in. He reined into the stable, stepped down from the saddle, and took care of the horse before leaving. He staggered as he started along the street, and paused at the door of the gun shop before entering. He glanced down at the floor where Wes Santee had fallen. It seemed like a bad dream now. He looked up at

Amos Berry, who was standing behind the counter.

'I'm sorry about what happened in here this afternoon, Amos,' Clay said. 'Santee was pushing it — I had to shoot him.'

'I know what happened, Clay,' Berry replied. 'You had no choice. I just hope your trouble is over now.'

'It ain't, not by a long rope.' Clay replied. 'Give me another box of forty-five shells, will you? I hope my credit is good.'

Berry picked up a box of cartridges and placed it on the counter. 'You can pay me any time,' he said.

Clay took the shells and departed, anxious now to see his father. The jail was next door to the gun shop and, as he paused at the street door of the law office, Clay heard the sound of hoofs along the street. He turned quickly, his right hand on the butt of his holstered gun. Two riders were coming towards him, and he felt a stab of relief strike through him when he recognized Bill

Cooper, the county sheriff, and Dave Swanston, who had gone to Sunset Ridge for the old lawman.

Cooper was past middle age, with a grizzled face which was more than half covered by a large, straggling grey moustache.

'Hold up there, Clay,' Cooper called. 'You can tell me what has been going on around here. Swanston wasn't sure about anything beyond the fact that you killed Wes Santee in the gun shop and had shot up half the town when he rode out to fetch me.'

Clay waited until the sheriff had dismounted and tied his horse to a nearby hitch rail before he opened the door of the office and entered with the sheriff behind him. Paul Edlin was seated at the desk with a shotgun in front of him. Edlin snatched up the weapon when he saw Clay, and then lowered it at the sight of the sheriff following behind.

'I'm sure glad to see you, Sheriff.' Edlin sprang to his feet. 'I don't know where Ritter is. I ain't seen him in two days. There's been a hell of a lot of trouble around here and I was left to handle it on my own. I've got Pete Overman in a cell, and I'm guarding him because Doc Miller said someone is out to kill him. I want you to know right now that I resign from standing in for the law whenever Ritter ain't around. I got my own business to handle. But before I go I want to tell you that I think Clay here should be in a cell. He did most of the shooting around town.'

'Sure. You get on about your business, Paul,' Cooper said. 'I'll handle this from here on in.' He sat down at the desk and looked pointedly at Edlin, who turned and departed swiftly, slamming the street door in leaving. 'Sit down, Clay, and tell me what you know. I heard that your ranch house was burned down yesterday. Start at the beginning and take me through the events, huh?'

'Let's take a look at my pa first,' Clay

suggested. 'Edlin said Pete is in a cell.'

'OK.' Cooper got up, looked around for the cell keys, and then led the way into the cell block. He paused on the threshold and Clay, glancing over the sheriff's shoulder, saw his father propped up on a bunk in a cell and holding a levelled pistol in his hand.

'Pa, what is going on?' Clay demanded.

Pete Overman grinned. His face was pale but his eyes glittered with grim determination. He lowered the pistol and heaved a sigh.

'It's good to see you, Clay. I've been worried about you. Thank God you've arrived, Bill,' he greeted the sheriff. 'We had to handle the law ourselves when Ritter turned bad.'

'So tell me about it.' Cooper entered the cell, which was unlocked, and sat down on the foot of the bunk.

Clay remained at the door of the cell, and was horrified when Pete described how Jake Moore had entered the doctor's bedroom to kill him. Cooper listened in silence and, when Pete ended his narrative by explaining that the doctor had brought him into the jail for safety before riding out with Sue Truscott because Big Frank had been shot, the sheriff nodded and turned to Clay.

'So what happened to you, Clay?' he demanded.

Clay heaved a sigh as he began to talk of the nightmare which had started when he found the stream dammed. Pete sat gripping his gun, nodding his head repeatedly as the grim events were unfolded. When Clay fell silent the sheriff nodded.

'So it looks like Mike Cade dreamed up all of this and Payne went along with it. Steve Garrett took a hand with Santee and Moore, and Ritter has mixed himself in with them. I think I've got the rights of it.' Cooper got to his feet. 'I'd better mosey over to FT and see how Big Frank is doing. Doc Miller is a good man, and if he took some posse men along with him then you can bet lead will be flying out at the ranch.

Doc is real hot on standing up for the law.'

'What about the bad men?' Pete asked. 'Cade and Payne have been running this, it looks like.'

'I'll arrest them if I see them.' Cooper eyed Clay. 'What do you reckon on doing now?'

'I don't think it is over yet, Sheriff,' Clay said grimly. 'Cade ain't likely to quit, and Payne has made his position clear. They can't back down. Then there are Garrett and Ritter. I reckon they've got to be arrested, or someone will have to kill them to stop them.'

'You may be right. Would you try to arrest them if you came up against them?'

'It's my fight,' Clay replied, 'and I'll do whatever is necessary to put an end to this trouble.'

'So hold up your right hand and I'll swear you in as my deputy. I'll need a good man around here until I get things under control again.'

Clay shook his head. 'I don't reckon

I'd be much use to you, Sheriff, and I've got a lot to do out at Bar O.'

'You won't be able to do anything until this trouble is settled one way or another,' Cooper replied. 'Come on, hold up your hand. I'll swear you in and then pin a badge on your chest.'

Clay grimaced. He was wondering where Cade was at that particular moment. Had the man come back to town? He looked into the sheriff's eyes and nodded slowly.

'OK, I'll try my hand at it. There are one or two things I ought to do. I think Mike Cade is in town and I figure to hunt him down.'

Cooper swore Clay in as a deputy and they went into the office. Cooper searched a drawer of the desk, produced a deputy badge, and pinned it to Clay's shirt front. He clapped a hand on Clay's shoulder and smiled reassuringly, but Clay was doubtful as he looked down at the badge.

'I'd better be on my way,' Cooper said. 'I'll take a look around FT and then come back here to back you up. Just keep your eyes open until I get back, huh? Let sleeping dogs lie.'

Clay nodded, locked the street door of the office behind the sheriff, and went in to the cell block to talk to Pete. His father seemed to be in considerable pain, but the pistol was in his hand and he was alert to his surroundings.

'You'd be more comfortable in the hotel, Pa,' Clay observed.

Pete shook his head. 'I'm doing all right in here. How long are you gonna wear that tin star?'

'When the sheriff gets back he'll make some other arrangements. I'll keep my eyes open for the men responsible for our trouble, and I'll arrest them if I can or kill them, whichever way they want it. Is there anything you need, Pa?'

'Not right now. All I want is to rest up until my shoulder heals. I — ' Pete broke off when he heard a hammering on the street door of the office, and lifted his pistol.

'Take it easy, Pa,' Clay advised. 'I'll see who it is.'

Clay went through to the office. He heard a voice outside, calling for Edlin to open the door, and drew his pistol when he recognized Ritter's voice. He unlocked the door, jerked it open, and stuck his gun in Ritter's stomach as the deputy pushed into the office. Ritter halted as if he had run into the side of a barn and gazed at Clay in amazement. Clay lifted a pistol from Ritter's holster. He noticed that the handcuffs he had put on Ritter's wrists earlier were still in place, but the connecting chain had been severed.

'Keep going through to the cells, Ritter,' Clay said tersely. 'I've got a cell booked specially for you.'

'What in hell are you doing in here?' Ritter demanded.

'Talk to the sheriff when he gets back,' Clay responded. 'Where are Cade and Payne?'

'Payne is all shot up. He had these handcuffs busted for me. I ain't seen

Cade. Payne and Garrett ain't pleased with Cade. He handled the business all wrong from the start. All he's done is get his men killed. I came back for my gear. I'm gonna split the breeze for other parts. I thought Edlin would be here. But I'll do a deal with you: I'll tell you where Cade is if you'll turn me loose.'

'No dice. Lead the way into the cells, Ritter.'

The crooked deputy gazed into Clay's face for several moments, then shrugged and walked through to the cells. He grimaced when he saw Pete in a cell, and gazed long and hard at the gun in Pete's hand. He raised no further objection when Clay thrust him into a nearby cell and then locked the iron door.

'Keep an eye on him, Pa,' Clay said. 'I'm gonna take a turn around the town. I've got a feeling Cade is here.'

'Watch your step, Clay,' Pete warned.

Clay nodded and departed. He locked the street door of the office and stood on the sidewalk looking around. Lights were showing in some of the windows fronting the street. He dropped a hand to his pistol as he walked along the sidewalk, peering into the shadows and alleys, and he was hair-triggered for trouble. He wondered where Cade had got to; a man who was practically a stranger in the county and had no friends. Clay shook his head, aware that there was little hope of tracking Cade down because he could be anywhere right now.

Clay could feel hunger gnawing at his insides and his throat was parched. He had been so occupied by the trouble since yesterday that he had been unable to take a respite. He went into Bennett's saloon and looked over the dozen men present. Edlin was standing at the bar talking angrily to the bar tender and Clay walked to the nearest end and called for a beer. He slaked his thirst and departed for the diner, aware that he would feel easier with a meal inside him.

After he had eaten he went out into the night and stood looking around. He was too conscious of the black cloud hanging over his head. There could be no rest for him until Cade was finished. He knew Cade would not give up his deadly intention of stealing range, and would have to be killed like a wild animal to bring about an end to the trouble. He went back to the law office nursing an uneasy gut-feeling that Cade was close by, probably awaiting an opportunity to kill off those ranged against him. He locked himself in the office, and sat at the desk with his chin on his chest, assailed by an overwhelming tiredness that enveloped him like a disease. His eyes seemed so heavy he could not keep them open, and he slept . . .

A fist pounding on the street door jerked him back to full awareness and he staggered as he arose from the desk. He drew his pistol and went to the door, fighting tiredness, and was surprised because he could see grey dawn pressing against the big front window. He unlocked the door to see Sheriff Cooper standing on the sidewalk, grinning tiredly.

'Come and give us a hand, Clay,' Cooper said. 'Doc has got Big Frank and Payne in a wagon and we need to get them into Doc's house for treatment. Doc reckons Big Frank will be OK, and Payne will recover to stand trial for his part in the trouble. Lock the door of the office and come along.'

Clay shook off the last vestiges of sleep and accompanied the sheriff to the doctor's house. He told the old lawman about Ritter showing up and being arrested. The sheriff was pleased, but he questioned Clay about the two bullet wounds Payne had collected.

'Did you use him for target practice?' Cooper asked.

Clay explained tersely, and added, 'It was Payne's leg or Sue's life, and the leg lost. Did you see any sign of Cade or Steve Garrett out at FT?'

Cooper shook his head. 'Nary a sign,'

he replied. 'I wouldn't be surprised if those two have upped stakes and made a run for it.'

'I don't think so. Cade wouldn't run. He's waiting for a chance to clean up around here.'

A wagon was pulled up outside Doc Miller's front door. Sue was sitting in the back beside Big Frank, who was conscious, his chest heavily bandaged. Payne was unconscious, with bandages on his leg and around his shoulder. Clay leaned on the side of the wagon and looked at Big Frank in the growing daylight.

'I'm glad you're pulling through, Frank,' Clay said.

'Sue told me what you've been doing, Clay. If it wasn't for you I wouldn't be alive and kicking now. You saved Sue from a lot of trouble. I owe you a big vote of thanks.'

Doc Miller emerged from his open doorway. He smiled at Clay, but when he looked around his expression changed swiftly and he reached for the pistol he was wearing in a holster on his right hip.

'Behind you, Clay,' Miller shouted.

Clay spun around, his hand dropping to his gun, and threw himself to the ground when he saw Cade and Steve Garrett standing at a corner of the house. Both were holding guns, and started shooting when the doctor called his warning. Clay thumbed back the hammer of his pistol, dimly aware that Sheriff Cooper had dropped to one knee beside him, his gun in his hand. Shots blasted, hurling thudding detonations across the peaceful town.

Cade's first shot smacked into the flesh of Clay's left side, about waist high. Clay triggered a reply as pain flared through his hip. He had eyes only for Cade, and saw his slug strike Cade in the centre of the chest. Cade twisted and fell heavily, dropping his gun, and the next instant Steve Garrett took two bullets in his chest — one from Doc Miller and the other from Sheriff Cooper. Clay dropped his gun and let his head fall onto his left arm. He lay unmoving while the echoes of the shooting faded.

Sue came running to his side and he lifted his head at the sound of her worried voice.

'I'm OK,' he said through clenched teeth. 'Cade won't bother us again. Maybe now we can pick up the pieces, huh?'

'Yes,' Sue said eagerly, grasping his hand. 'And between us we'll put our lives back together the way they should be.'

Clay nodded and relaxed. Sheriff Cooper was checking Cade and Garrett, and reported that both men were dead. Clay was satisfied. He had fought against big odds and won . . .

THE END

We do hope that you have enjoyed reading this large print book.

Did you know that all of our titles are available for purchase?

We publish a wide range of high quality large print books including:
Romances, Mysteries, Classics
General Fiction
Non Fiction and Westerns

Special interest titles available in large print are:
The Little Oxford Dictionary
Music Book, Song Book
Hymn Book, Service Book

Also available from us courtesy of Oxford University Press:
Young Readers' Dictionary
(large print edition)
Young Readers' Thesaurus
(large print edition)

For further information or a free brochure, please contact us at:
Ulverscroft Large Print Books Ltd.,
The Green, Bradgate Road, Anstey,
Leicester, LE7 7FU, England.
Tel: (00 44) **0116 236 4325**
Fax: (00 44) **0116 234 0205**

LOPEZ'S LOOT

David Bingley

They were cousins, riding partners: Drifter, a white American, and Lopez — half-Mexican, travelling the southern border trails of the USA. Their money-raising schemes were often shady, sharing the risks and rewards: like the time Drifter turned in his 'wanted' partner, Lopez, and later sprung him. However, things changed when loot, in the form of church treasures, came their way. Clashing with posses and renegades their lives were at risk. Could they ever gain a more settled way of life?

THE DEATH SHADOW RIDERS

Elliot Conway

Bank robber Jake Larribee saves Blaze Morgan from a cattleman's hanging. But then Blaze's handiness with his pistol lands them in deeper trouble. And whilst being beholden to a sutler and his daughter, they take on the biggest rancher in southern New Mexico, Simpson and his crew of the Slash Y ranch. Allied with three Mexican boys and their grandpappy, they begin a guerrilla war against the Slash Y — a war destined to end in one final bloodletting shoot-out.

GUNTRAIL TO CONDOR

John Glasby

Seth Claybourne, a defeated Confederate soldier with no reason to return home, decided to ride west. Crossing a desert he encountered a man who had been left for dead. Jeb Dawson was still alive, but when his attackers returned, Seth drove them off. Dawson, unfit to travel, wanted Seth to travel to Condor Peaks to validate his claim on valuable land. Vested interests wanted him dead. And being Dawson's proxy put Seth into the firing line . . .

RIO BONITO

Abe Dancer

Joe Kettle needs all the grit he's inherited from his father and his father before him: Wilshaw Broome, formerly of the Standing K ranch, has hired gunmen to seize Kettle's domain. Joe sets out to regain his birthright with Hector Chaf and Ben McGovren — each one with reason for facing overwhelming opposition . . . They'll play a waiting game, use hidden trails along the Rio Bonito and, when the time is right, they'll meet force with force and guns with guns.

Síscéalta Lios Lurgain

An Chéad Eagrán 2015
© Aoife Ní Dhufaigh 2015

ISBN 978-1-909907-97-3

*Ní thagraíonn aon phearsa ficseanúil sa scéal seo
d'aon duine sa saol réadúil.*

Clóchur, dearadh agus ealaín: Caomhán Ó Scolaí

Clódóireacht: Clódóirí Lurgan

Foras na Gaeilge

Tugann Foras na Gaeilge tacaíocht airgid do Leabhar Breac

Tugann An Chomhairle Ealaíon tacaíocht airgid do Leabhar Breac

Leabhar Breac, Indreabhán, Co. na Gaillimhe.
Teil: 091-593592